"Do you trust me, Amelia?"

Cole watched Amelia's face. He knew by looking at her what she was going through. Her expression mirrored her feelings as they churned and morphed inside her. She'd gone from shock to disbelief to doubt to uncertainty.

And that's where she was right now. She wasn't sure if she could believe everything he'd just told her, much less trust him.

He understood perfectly. The mission depended on whether he was telling the truth. But he couldn't tell her everything. Not yet. For her own safety and the safety of the people of Raven's Cliff.

"I don't have a choice, do I?"

"You always have a choice."

He watched her and waited, knowing how much depended on her answer.

"I'll trust you, Cole Robinson."

He nodded in relief, proud of her for being so brave.

Knowing full well he had no choice either: he had to trust her.

CAST OF CHARACTERS

Cole Robinson – This undercover Homeland Security Agent will sacrifice his life if necessary to stop a ruthless domestic terrorist. But when his mission endangers a brave and vulnerable young woman and her town, Cole discovers he has something to live for.

Amelia Hopkins – She's dedicated her life to her father and to Hopkins Boat Works. But when she's abducted by a mysterious stranger who's in league with terrorists, Amelia's life – and heart – are turned upside down.

Reginald Hopkins – Amelia's father is a brilliant designer, but since his heart attack he hasn't created a new yacht design. With Reginald unable to carry out Chien Fou's plan, will his life and the lives of everyone in Raven's Cliff be forfeit?

The Fortune Teller – Who is this mysterious woman who knows everything about Cole and Amelia, and whose cryptic words prophesy love – or doom?

Chien Fou – The ruthless domestic terrorist who has named himself "Mad Dog" plans to destroy America's economy, and anyone who impedes him risks his very life.

Ross Fancher – This ambitious young man is interested in Amelia, but he's in Chien Fou's way.

Mayor Wells – His political ambitions have put him in the pockets of criminals and have endangered the town. Now it appears he's in league with the terrorists. Is he ready to sacrifice the town and even his daughter to gain his own ends?

Camille Wells – The mayor's daughter is in a coma, watched over not only by her parents, but by a shadowy figure who only shows up in the dark of night.

Solving the Mysterious Stranger

MALLORY KANE

MILLS & BOON®

Pure reading pleasure™

*First published in Great Britain 2009
by Harlequin Mills & Boon Limited,
Eton House, 18-24 Paradise Road, Richmond, Surrey TW9 1SR*

© Harlequin Books S.A. 2008

*Special thanks and acknowledgement to Mallory Kane for her
contribution to the CURSE OF RAVEN'S CLIFF mini-series.*

ISBN: 978 0 263 87297 2

46-0609

*Harlequin Mills & Boon policy is to use papers that are
natural, renewable and recyclable products and made from
wood grown in sustainable forests. The logging and
manufacturing processes conform to the legal environmental
regulations of the country of origin.*

*Printed and bound in Spain
by Litografia Rosés S.A., Barcelona*

ABOUT THE AUTHOR

Mallory Kane credits her love of books to her mother, a librarian, who taught her that books are a precious resource and should be treated with loving respect. Her father and grandfather were steeped in the southern tradition of oral history, and could hold an audience spellbound for hours with their storytelling skills. Mallory aspires to be as good a storyteller as her father.

She loves romantic suspense with dangerous heroes and dauntless heroines, and often uses her medical background to add an extra dose of intrigue to her books. Another fascination that she enjoys exploring in her reading and writing is the infinite capacity of the brain to adapt and develop higher skills.

Mallory lives in Mississippi with her computer-genius husband, their two fascinating cats, and, at current count, seven computers.

She loves to hear from readers. You can write to her at mallory@mallorykane.com.

For Allison and the great group of authors with
whom I was privileged to work.

Chapter One

"There is a pall cast over this town. Your destiny and the destiny of Raven's Cliff are entwined like lovers."

Amelia Hopkins tried to pull her hand away from the fortune-teller's red-tipped fingers, but the woman's grip was surprisingly strong.

"Maybe you haven't heard," Amelia said, "but the Seaside Strangler is dead and the poisoned fish are gone. Even the mayor's daughter, who's been missing for months, has been found alive. There is no *pall*."

As she talked, she studied the woman's face, trying to see beneath the layers of stage makeup. She was surprised that she didn't recognize her. She knew almost everyone in Raven's Cliff.

"I thought you were going to tell me about meeting the man of my dreams."

Her friends Carrie and Rita had come out of the fortune-teller's shadowy booth with promises of love and marriage, beautiful babies and happily-ever-after. No warnings of doom and gloom. No ominous, cryptic predictions.

Amelia had tried to refuse to have her fortune read. But her friends had insisted.

Fortune-tellers. Crystal balls. Palm reading. All woo-woo tricks designed to provide a moment's distraction and to part people from their hard-earned money.

Although she'd loaned the mayor's assistant her stage makeup case, which had seen years of use in the small dinner theater in town and had funded a large part of the boat festival, she'd refused to play fortune-teller.

She didn't have time for such nonsense. She had a business to run.

The fortune-teller's pale blue eyes sparkled in the flickering candlelight as she stared deeply into her crystal ball. She waved a hand near one of the candles and a faint scent of roses drifted past Amelia's nostrils.

"Okay, I give up," Amelia said. "Who are you? Are you in town just for the festival? Did the mayor hire you?"

The woman frowned at her before dropping her gaze back to the orb. "I am Tatiana. I do not know what you mean." She held a hand over the ball, close—but not touching it.

Amelia could imagine sparks of electricity arcing from the woman's hand to the crystal sphere. She was a good actress.

"Okay then, Tatiana. Hurry up and tell me about my soul mate. I've got to get home."

"Word in the town is that *nobody* is good enough for you, Amelia Hopkins. And yet I say, you *will* find your soul mate. It is part of your destiny. But he is not the man of your dreams—" The fortune-teller paused. "For you, the journey to love will be a long one, and fraught with danger." She took Amelia's hand.

"You must prepare yourself, for death hovers over you as surely as it does over Raven's Cliff. Your only hope is your own wit. Take care whom you trust."

A sudden chill breeze sent shadows racing along the walls like bats and extinguished several candles. The smell of hot wax mingled with the aroma of roses.

Amelia tried to pull her hand away, but the woman's scarlet-tipped fingers held tight.

"Remember this, Amelia. Pay heed to a dark, mysterious stranger with eyes like storm clouds and a haunted past."

Oh, please. Sure—Raven's Cliff had experienced more than its share of tragedy, but the deadly summer was over. Autumn had arrived. Foggy mornings and crisp, clear afternoons were a refreshing change after the sweltering, awful summer.

"Appearances can be deceiving. Look not with your eyes but with your heart."

Amelia uttered a short laugh. That was more like it. Platitudes she could share with Carrie and Rita. "Right. Got it."

She stood and firmly pulled her hand away. "A mysterious stranger, a path *fraught* with danger and deceit. Great," she said wryly. "I can't wait."

Quelling the urge to wipe her hand on her jeans, she dug into her pocket and came up with a wad of twenties. Peeling off two, she dropped them onto the table.

"Nice special effects." She turned and reached for the heavy curtain that draped the front of the booth.

"Wait!" The dozens of bangles on the woman's

wrists chimed. "That case on the table there, it's yours. You should take it with you. Keep it close—you're going to need it."

So it *was* her makeup the fake fortune-teller had used. She grabbed up the case.

"And, Amelia Hopkins…"

She paused—only inches from freedom. "Aren't you done yet?"

"Remember. *Nobody* is good enough for you."

Amelia shook her head and pushed through the curtain, just in time to run into a solid wall of flesh.

"Oh, sorry," she muttered, putting out her hands to steady herself as the man grasped her waist.

She pushed against him, but he held on. "Let me go," she demanded, slightly alarmed by his unrelenting hold.

He loomed over her, dark and ominous. A few days' growth of beard darkened his square jaw. A black wool fisherman's cap shadowed the upper part of his face. But no shadows could hide the steely gray of his eyes.

Something flickered in those eyes—curiosity? Recognition? Then he let go of her and held up his hands, palms out. He ducked his head, letting the brim of his cap shadow the upper part of his face. "Beg pardon, ma'am," he muttered.

Amelia pushed past him.

"Ma'am, you dropped this."

She turned.

He knelt and picked up her makeup case. She must have dropped it when he collided with her.

He held it out.

She took it, but before she could thank him, he'd turned away, moving off through the crowd. His black leather jacket strained across his shoulders, and his long legs looked powerful in black wool pants. He was taller than most of the people around him, and yet he moved with the fluid grace of a big cat.

"Amelia," Carrie Singleton called, waving.

Amelia pulled her gaze away from the stranger's leather-clad shoulders in time to see Carrie duck around a clown who looked suspiciously like Hal Smith, the owner of the hardware store. He blew an obnoxiously loud whistle.

Rita Maxwell laughed as she followed Carrie.

"What did the fortune-teller say?" Carrie asked.

"You weren't in there long enough," Rita said, eyeing her suspiciously. "You just gave her some money and left, didn't you?"

"No." Amelia gestured down the street in the direction the stranger had gone. "Did you see the way that guy grabbed me?"

"A guy grabbed you?" Rita asked.

Amelia gestured, but he'd disappeared into the crowd. "You couldn't miss him. He grabbed me and wouldn't let go. I was about to scream for help."

Carrie glanced down the street and frowned.

Rita shook her head. "I saw you bump into someone—tall guy with shoulders out to here—but you barely brushed each other."

"He's probably a sailor, docked here for Boat Fest," Rita added. "I'm sure you're the prettiest thing he's seen in six months."

Amelia stared at her two friends. "I'm telling you he wouldn't let go. And he didn't look like a sailor. He looked like a—" *A captain,* she thought.

"Come on. Let's go get an Irish coffee. I want to hear what the fortune-teller told you." Carrie hooked her arm through Amelia's and pulled her in the direction of The Pub—the direction the stranger had gone.

Amelia glanced at her watch. "If I have a drink, I'll fall asleep standing up. I've been hawking yachts all day and my feet are killing me. I should be getting home. Dad and I have an early meeting tomorrow and we need to coordinate our talking points."

"It's not even ten o'clock. Honestly, you're like an old maid sometimes," Rita said.

"Yeah." Carrie guided Amelia through the weathered cherrywood doors of The Pub. "The richest, most gorgeous old maid on the entire coast. Not to mention the A-Number-One party pooper."

"Carrie, stop it." Amelia chuckled. "I'll have some coffee—regular, decaf coffee, but then I've got to go home. Hopkins Yachts doesn't run itself. Especially not during Boat Fest—and especially not this year." She didn't specify that the main reason she needed to be at home was to make sure her father got to bed by eleven o'clock.

"Did you get a lot of orders at the boat show?"

"Yes. Too many. That's what this meeting tomorrow is about. Some megacorporation wants to meet with Dad about a major contract."

"That's great," Carrie commented absently as they picked their way through the crowd.

The Seafarer Boat Fest attracted a lot of people—tourists, sailors, yachting enthusiasts who came to see Hopkins's newest designs.

Amelia felt a faint prick of guilt. Hopkins's preview

drawings for next year's designs were a myth. There was no inspired new Hopkins yacht for the coming year. Probably only a seasoned aficionado would notice, but Amelia still felt as if they were cheating their customers.

Since her father's heart attack a year ago, he hadn't created one new workable design. That was bad enough. But he'd insisted that no one know that this year's new designs were glossed-over versions from the past three years.

Even worse, this year's Boat Fest had drawn more people than usual—many of them curiosity-seekers who'd heard about all the trouble Raven's Cliff had experienced throughout the summer. But as was true every year, a lot were boaters looking for the latest fancy yacht.

Everywhere Amelia went, she steeled herself for the accusation she knew would come one day—*Reginald Hopkins has lost it. He's recycling old designs and calling them new.*

As they pushed through the crowd toward the bar, the bartender, Seamus Hannigan, nodded a greeting. His eyes crinkled at the corners, which pulled at the scar that ran from his chin up his jawline. His gaze followed Carrie.

Amelia poked her friend in the ribs.

"Stop it." Carrie slapped at her hand.

"Seamus is looking your way. Wink at him and get us a table."

Rita chuckled.

"I mean it, Amelia," Carrie said. "I'm totally not interested. I've never winked at a man and I'm sure not going to start now."

But even in the dim, smoky pub, Amelia didn't miss Carrie's flaming cheeks. She caught Rita's eye. "Let's sit at the bar then."

"There are only two seats," Carrie protested.

"I'll stand," Rita said.

"I won't be here long enough to sit," Amelia said at the same time.

They pushed through the crowd. Amelia guided Carrie to one empty chair and shot a look at Rita. With a shake of her blonde head, Rita sat next to Carrie.

"I'll have a decaf coffee," Amelia told Rita, and glanced around. The atmosphere in the pub was cheerful—almost frantically so. Everyone was celebrating, and they had a right to, after the tragic summer.

The din of conversation occasionally yielded up a coherent sentence fragment, most involving the mayor. Amelia closed her eyes and listened.

"—ought to be kicked out of office. He took kickbacks while people were dying from the fish poison."

"—older folks are convinced the curse is back."

"—got to admit he stepped up—"

"—then I said there's no such thing as ghosts—"

"Well, I feel sorry for him. He almost lost his daughter."

Amelia's heart ached at the reminder that while the town was celebrating, her best friend Camille, Mayor Wells's daughter, was lying helpless in a coma.

No matter what the mayor had done, he loved his daughter. Amelia knew that. He'd just let his greed get the better of him.

The townsfolk were divided—either condemning him for taking bribes or forgiving him because he'd done it for his only child.

He'd tried to make up for his actions. He'd worked hard to beef up Raven's Cliff's annual Seafarer Boat Fest to celebrate the end of the nightmarish summer.

The television mounted over the bar was tuned to the local news station. They were replaying Mayor Wells's speech from earlier in the evening. His face looked pale and drawn, and his smile seemed pasted on as he praised the townspeople for their bravery and expressed sorrow for the four lovely young women who had died at the hands of the Seaside Strangler.

As he mentioned their names, their photos flashed on the screen. Amelia hadn't known Rebecca Johnson or Cora McDonald, and had only met Angela Wheeler once, but Sofia Lagios was Detective Andrei Lagios's baby sister. Seeing her fresh, beautiful face sent a pang of sorrow through Amelia's heart.

As the mayor's prerecorded voice encouraged the townspeople to enjoy the fireworks show, Rita pressed a steaming mug topped with whipped cream into Amelia's hands.

A cheer rose above the low murmur of voices in The Pub. Quite a few people stood and raised their glasses to the TV.

Amelia followed suit then took a sip. *Irish whiskey.* She frowned. Rita had handed her the wrong mug.

At that moment a pair of stone-cold gray eyes caught her gaze.

Eyes like storm clouds. It was *him.* The stranger who'd run into her. He held a beer. Instead of raising his glass to the TV and the crowd, he saluted her.

She wanted to look away—ignore him. But he was a man who could never be ignored. Her first impression of him still held—he wasn't a sailor, not even a first mate—if he were on a ship, he'd be the captain.

Pay heed to a dark, mysterious stranger with eyes like storm clouds and a haunted past.

The fortune-teller's words echoed in Amelia's ears. She shivered.

As if he could read her mind, he nodded, such a brief gesture she might have imagined it, then his wide, straight mouth tilted slightly at one corner. He saluted her again and lifted his glass to his lips.

A hand touched her shoulder.

She started.

"Amelia. You're jumpy tonight," a familiar gravelly voice said.

"Uncle Marvin, you sneaked up on me." Amelia smiled at her father's friend and mentor. Marvin Smith wasn't her uncle, but he'd been like a father to her dad after his parents died.

"How are you doing?"

Marvin sighed. "I'll be fine when the town is back to normal. Is your dad around?"

She shook her head, ignoring the beguiling urge to look back in the direction of the gray-eyed stranger. "He's at home, still recovering from that flu bug. I wouldn't let him come. Mrs. Winston is keeping him supplied with chicken soup and hot tea."

Marvin shook his grizzled head. "Is he going to be able to meet with those people tomorrow?"

Amelia almost smiled at the derision in his voice. *Those people* were a highly respected maritime organization who wanted to commission a fleet of fishing vessels from Hopkins Yachts.

"He'll be ready," she said airily. She wanted so badly to tell Uncle Marvin about her dad's illness, but Reginald Hopkins wasn't willing to let anyone know about his heart attack and his resulting inability to design a new yacht. Not even his beloved mentor.

She looked at her watch. "I need to get home. We're getting up at six o'clock to make the trip into Bangor for the meeting."

Marvin's thick brows drew down as he scowled. "Well, tell Reg to take his medicine and I'll see him soon."

Medicine. "Oh, no! I forgot."

She reached around Carrie and set her mug on the bar. "I've got to find Frank. I was supposed to pick up a prescription refill this afternoon."

"Frank's still at his shop." Marvin jerked a thumb toward the south. "I saw him in there just a little while ago. He said he had a couple more prescriptions to fill before he turned in."

"Great. I'll see you later, Uncle Marvin." She put a hand on each of her friends' shoulders. "Girls, I've got to run to the pharmacy before I go home. I'll talk to you two tomorrow, okay?"

"Amelia, wait!" Rita stood and caught her forearm. "The midnight fireworks show is going to be better than the earlier one. Stay and watch it with us."

"I can't. I'll see it from the cliff house." Amelia gave Rita a hug and pressed her cheek against Carrie's. "Have a good time."

She glanced at her watch as she pushed through the crowd. Eleven-thirty. The street was packed with people waiting for the fireworks. Tired children drooped in their laughing parents' arms. Teens and adults alike filled the air with the din of noisemakers and whistles, and even some of the town's most prominent citizens sloshed beer and shouted welcome to tourists.

Looking down the street, she saw lights in the pharmacy's window. Thank goodness Frank was still working. He usually closed up at 9:00 p.m. She supposed he'd stayed open because of the festival.

Her dad was completely out of his arrhythmia medication. If she didn't get his prescription tonight, neither of them would make the meeting tomorrow. He couldn't miss a single dose, or his heart would start beating too fast to pump blood. And without blood flow to his heart, he'd die.

COLE ROBINSON SET his half-full beer mug down on the table. Amelia Hopkins had left The Pub. He'd seen her mahogany-colored hair swinging as the heavy wood door closed behind her.

"Hold it, Robinson," his tablemate growled. "Where d'ya think you're going? You haven't finished your beer."

"None of your business," he growled right back. "I'll see you later."

"The excitement's just about to get started. We're supposed to be ready to—you know, as soon as the fireworks start. Leader said so."

Cole pulled the brim of his cap down. "Yeah? Well he gave me my own orders."

"Your own—?"

Cole pushed past another couple of sailors and headed out the door. He ducked his head and stuck his hands in the pockets of his black leather jacket. Hunching his shoulders, he tried to appear inches shorter than his six-feet-two as he glanced up and down the street.

He'd been in town two days, following Amelia Hopkins, getting to know her habits. He'd already figured out she was a workaholic.

She'd spent at least twenty-four hours of the past forty-eight down at the boatyard below the architectural phenomenon that was Reginald Hopkins's house. The locals called it the Cliff House. Cole glanced upward. Built into the side of a cliff, away from the lighthouse and south of the town proper, Hopkins's house was faced with local rock. On first inspection it appeared to be a part of the cliff face. In fact, if it weren't for the elevator that must have been added recently, the house would be all but invisible.

Cole spotted Amelia a few stores down, lit by all the Boat Fest lights. She knocked on a glass door, then entered. The *Rx* symbol above the door told him it was a pharmacy. He headed in that direction, curious to know what she needed from the drugstore.

What did a rich, beautiful heiress to a vast boat-building fortune need from a small-town pharmacy?

Birth-control pills? Allergy medication? Something more serious? Cole had dug up everything he could find about her, which was quite a lot. She'd lived a life of privilege and fame, being the daughter of one of the East Coast's most famous yacht designers.

From everything he'd seen and learned, she was the very picture of health. Dewy skin, shiny, bouncy hair, unusual honey-colored eyes and a mouth that was made for smiling—and kissing.

Hell. Where had that thought come from? Sure she

was gorgeous, with a supple, delicately muscled body that spoke to years of climbing on the cliffs and sailing along the rocky coastline. But he had no business thinking of her like that. She was an assignment. An innocent victim about to be caught up in a heinous domestic terrorist plot.

It was his bad luck that ever since the first moment he'd laid eyes on her, he couldn't get her out of his head or figure her out.

For instance, why had a no-nonsense business-woman like her agreed to pose for a mildly risqué calendar? She didn't look at all like her photos in the new Hopkins Boatworks calendar he'd picked up at the last port.

The woman in those pictures was a sexual being—sizzling in forties-style clothes and makeup. She'd been photographed in black and white, standing in front of next year's model of luxury yacht presented in full color.

If he didn't know better, he wouldn't believe they were the same person. Even though the woman in the calendar was definitely a turn-on, for some reason he preferred her like this. Serious, straight and trim, with her hair loose and swinging about her shoulders.

What he had to do bothered him—a lot. Enough that he'd followed an impulse he never should have considered, much less acted on. If his abrupt decision backfired, it could blow the plan that had taken months to set in motion.

And blowing the plan at this stage would be a deadly mistake.

Not to mention that he was two hundred dollars poorer,

with no idea whether his money had been wasted. He'd paid the fortune-teller to embellish Amelia's fortune.

But had she?

"Tell her to be careful," he'd instructed the woman. "Can you somehow let her know she can trust me?"

The fortune-teller had looked at the wad of twenties and then at him. She'd frowned. "You are caught between two worlds."

"Yeah—look, lady. Don't tell *my* fortune. I know mine. Tell hers. She's on her way here now. You just finished with her two friends."

"No. Wait a moment. You must listen to me. You live in two different worlds, and those worlds are about to collide. You must be extremely careful or your young woman may be crushed in the collision."

"Great." He'd tossed another wad of twenties down and turned up his nose at the smell of spice and roses drifting up from a dish on the table. "Sounds good. I'm going out through the back."

As he left, she'd called out to him. "Listen for my voice. I will guide you as much as possible. But only if you open your mind and heart."

Back on the street, Cole had muttered a curse. That was two hundred dollars ill-spent. He figured the fortune-teller was already pocketing the bills and planning to get as much from Amelia as she could.

A couple passed him, walking arm-in-arm, drawing his thoughts back to the present. They glanced at him with idle curiosity.

He half turned away and pretended to light an invisible cigarette with a nonexistent lighter.

The high-school band struck up a march, and the

chatter and cheers grew louder as the twelve-o'clock hour approached.

Cole's pulse sped up. The fireworks would begin in a few minutes. He needed to be done with his task before his new buddies began theirs.

The sound of an old-fashioned bell signaled Amelia's exit from the pharmacy. She called out her thanks to the pharmacist as the door closed behind her and the bell's ring faded. She turned south, away from the town square.

She was going home. She walked with a bounce in her step. She didn't know her life was about to change forever.

He followed at a careful distance, wishing he wasn't fascinated by the way her jeans cupped her bottom and emphasized her long legs, wishing her hair wasn't so shiny that it caught the light of the moon, wishing he was someone else—and so was she.

As soon as she left the lights of town behind and started climbing the cliff path, Cole lengthened his stride. His soft-soled boots made almost no noise on the rocky road. In contrast, her leather soles clicked loudly against the stones and gravel. She wasn't dressed for speed, not with those ridiculous high-heeled boots on.

The sky lit up. *The fireworks.* Time to make his move.

In three long strides he caught up with her, just as she slowed for a glance back at the display. He wrapped one arm all the way around her, pinning her body against him.

She didn't make a sound, just stiffened. Then she kicked and twisted, trying to break his hold.

Behind him, firecrackers cracked and rockets whistled. The sky flashed like lightning.

"Don't use up your energy struggling. You're going to need it." He grabbed both her wrists in one hand and slipped his other hand around her neck from behind.

He didn't squeeze. He just let his fingers trail along her larynx. He felt more than heard her suck in a deep breath.

"Don't scream," he muttered. "I can break your neck before you can make a sound."

Chapter Two

Amelia's throat moved against Cole's fingers as she swallowed.

"I don't scream," she hissed, her words a lot braver than her voice.

Her bravado made him angry.

Damn it, Amelia, don't be stupid. Stupid people often didn't live long enough to regret their actions.

"Do you cry?" he growled. "Because I can break your fingers one at a time *and* keep you conscious so you can feel each bone crack."

Her head jerked. He'd gotten to her. She might not scream, might not even fear death, but she *did* fear pain.

"You are talented, aren't you?" she retorted, her voice hoarse with the strain of staying calm.

He almost smiled through his anger. Her courage was ill-aimed, but she had plenty of it. "Don't mess with me, sweetheart. You're making me angry, and I promise you won't like me when I'm angry."

"I don't like you now." She swallowed again, stronger this time. "What do you want from me?"

He ignored her question. "Pick up that case you dropped. I don't want anything to look out of place."

He loosed his hold long enough for her to scoop up the case, and then he nudged her forward. "Move it."

Unexpectedly, she twisted, trying to break his grip. Instinctively, he jerked her back.

She gasped.

"Don't try that again. I promise you'll regret it. I can knock you out if I have to."

"Wow. Is there no end to what you can do?"

"You've got me beat at stand-up comedy." He scowled. She was afraid, but her wisecracks taunted him. He had to watch himself. This wasn't a silly flirtation, nor a prelude to a date. It was an abduction—a deadly serious business.

He couldn't afford to lose sight of his goal for one second.

They came to a fork in the gravel road. If he continued up toward her house, the rocks would block his view of the harbor, and he needed to see the boats. So he pushed her in the other direction, down toward the Hopkins's boatyard.

"Where…are you taking me?"

He knew what she was thinking. From the moment he'd first heard about Amelia Hopkins and the Global Freedom Front's plans, her fate had haunted him— that's why he'd gone to their leader and requested this job.

Thank God he'd earned the terrorist leader's respect. It had taken him three years, but he'd finally managed to get close enough to Chien Fou to ensure that whatever he asked for, he got.

The idea that one of his fellow seamen might lay his hands on Amelia sickened Cole. Yet he knew that in the deepest, most shameful corner of his soul, the idea of taking her, willingly or not, titillated him.

He disgusted himself.

"Look, whoever you are. I have money. Lots of it," she said desperately. "I'll make sure you're set for life. Just please don't—"

"Shut up!" he snapped.

Off to the north, the boats were moving. Amelia spotted them as soon as he did. She stopped.

"What's going on down there?"

The boats were rigged like pirate ships, flying the Jolly Roger. Cole heard cheers and laughter coming from the little town below.

Chien Fou's ruse had worked. Cole pictured exactly what the townsfolk saw.

Ships with black sails and orange pirate flags. Seamen with red rags around their heads and knives in their teeth.

"Oh, dear heavens," Amelia whispered, and craned her neck to look up at him.

He met her gaze for the third time and, just like the first, when he'd put himself in her path as she came out of the fortune-teller's booth, and the second in the crowded pub, her eyes glowed like Tupelo honey.

Her expression morphed from puzzlement to confusion to horror within the space of a second.

"You!" she stormed.

He nodded and curved his mouth in what he hoped was a sneer. "You don't look like the type who'd pay a fortune-teller. What'd she tell you—beware of strangers?"

Two spots of crimson flared across her cheekbones. His pulse jumped. So the fortune-teller had gotten his message across. Or spilled the beans about the weird guy and his odd request.

"What's going on down there? Who are they?" Her head jerked toward the boats.

"Who knows? Pirates. Revelers. Paid performers." He heard the sting in his own voice.

"No, they're not."

She was entirely too intuitive.

"They're not part of the festival. Something's happening. Something bad." She surprised him by jerking against his thumb, a classic self-defense move. She took off running.

Damn it. He threw himself after her. She was nimble and quick, skipping down the cliff-side path, her high heels clicking on the rocks.

Then suddenly she went down. Her fancy boots were her undoing, just as he'd predicted.

He caught up to her in no time. She lay in an awkward heap on a jutting rock, her eyes glittering like gold nuggets—or hot coals.

Cole examined the line of her body. Was she hurt? Or was she feigning? At this point, he wouldn't put anything past her.

Then he saw it. The long skinny heel of her boot appeared caught under a rock.

"I knew I should have brought my purse. I carry a gun. I could have shot you."

"No purse? Then what's this?" he asked, picking up the metal case she kept dropping when she fell.

"Give me that."

He examined it. "What is it?"

"Nothing you'd be interested in."

He flipped the clasp and opened it. "Makeup?"

"Stage makeup. Some of the performers used it."

"The fortune-tellers." He thought about the boat calendar and her perfect 1940s makeup and hair. "You're an actress?"

"None of your business. May I have my case?"

He handed her the case.

She kicked him.

"Ow! Damn it!" Her spiked heel made a big dent in his forearm. She jabbed at him again. He grabbed her foot. "Stop!"

"Oh! You're breaking my ankle."

"Yeah. Right." He was barely touching her, but he held his hands up, palms out. "Get up."

Amelia glared at the bully who had abducted her. She couldn't let him know how terrified she was. When he'd grabbed her earlier, she'd seen the hastily disguised lust in his eyes.

She'd always been capable of taking care of herself. Plus her father's employees had always looked after her like family.

But there was no one around to protect her now. This dangerous stranger had anticipated every move she'd made.

Whatever he wanted to do to her, she'd be helpless against him.

What an idiot she was, wearing these ridiculous thousand-dollar boots. She should have worn her hiking boots. Of course her plans for the evening hadn't included being hauled up and down the cliff face by a ruffian.

"Let's go. I said, get up." He held out his hand. It was a large hand, with short blunt fingernails. His palm was calloused—she'd felt its roughness against her neck.

She lowered her gaze. If he looked into her eyes, he'd know she was planning something. She figured she had one last chance to get away.

She took his hand and moved to stand, mentally rehearsing her rash, spur-of-the-moment plan. If she could surprise him and throw him off balance, she could escape and warn the town—of what exactly, she had no idea. But she knew that those pirate boats converging on the harbor boded ill for Raven's Cliff.

She feinted as if she'd lost her footing, then with all her might she swung the makeup case at his head.

He stopped her so easily it was laughable. He wrenched the case from her hands.

"Nice trick. Try it on someone your own size. I'll hold on to this. I don't care to be banged on the head with it. Now let's go. We need to head up to your house now. You can walk or I can carry you. It's your choice."

Amelia glared at him. Helplessness churned in her gut until she felt ill. She had no chance of escaping him. None.

Whatever he wanted, he'd take.

"What do you want from me if it's not money?"

He didn't answer, just tilted his head back an inch and raked her body with his gaze.

Amelia's heart pounded in her ears as fear wrapped icy fingers around her heart. He *was* going to rape her, or kill her or both. Everyone in Raven's Cliff was convinced the Seaside Strangler was dead. But what if this man—

"Look. I'm not talking pocket change. I've got enough to set you up for life. I'll give you whatever you want." She sounded pathetic, but she didn't care.

Gone was her bravado, gone the self-assurance and determination that made her a good businesswoman.

She did not want to die.

The last of the fireworks exploded, lighting up the sky. The stranger's head jerked.

Instinctively, Amelia whirled and took off running. She got nowhere. He grabbed her belt loop and pulled her back.

"I told you we're going up the hill—one way or another. I guess it's going to be *another*." He turned her around and cupped his hand behind her ear.

And that was all she knew.

SOMEBODY WAS POUNDING on her forehead. She felt dizzy and disoriented, as if the world had flipped upside down.

Her forehead bumped against a hard surface. She opened her eyes and squinted.

The world wasn't upside down. *She was.* She was hanging over the stranger's shoulder like a duffel bag. The position squeezed her chest so she could hardly get a full breath.

She squirmed.

"Be still." He moved his hand from her thighs to her bottom.

"Put me down," she whispered angrily as she squirmed some more, only to discover that the pressure of her breasts against his shoulder was causing them to tighten. The tingling awareness slid all the way through her.

Fear, she told herself. That's all it was. Only, the heat of his hand on her butt didn't feel scary. It felt protective—and tingly.

"Put me down! Now!" She pounded on his back with her fists and kicked, working to bury the toes of her boots in his flesh. Nothing fazed him, but she kept on anyhow.

He doggedly trudged ahead. She heard his hard, steady breathing and felt the tense bands of his shoulder muscles under her breasts.

Within seconds she was exhausted. Her limbs burned with effort. She was ready to cry. She'd never felt so helpless in her life. And yet she knew with dreaded certainty that this was only the beginning of what this stranger had in store for her.

"I…don't know what…you think you're…doing but…you're not going to…get away…with it." It was a struggle just to breathe, let alone talk, with her chest bouncing on the ball of his shoulder.

He didn't answer.

With a great effort, Amelia lifted her head, peering down at the town below. The shouts of celebration had stopped. Now the night was eerily silent and dark in the shadows of the new moon.

Something awful had happened.

She racked her brain for a way to escape the stranger before they got to her house. She'd do anything to keep him away from her father.

"Stop! Now!" she demanded desperately, with no hope that he'd pay any attention to her.

To her surprise he stopped. Then he dumped her off his shoulder. Her legs collapsed beneath her.

"Please," she gasped. "Tell me what you want."

He held out his hand like a gentleman. She wanted to spit on it, but she quelled that childish urge and took his hand, allowing him to pull her upright.

When she raised her gaze to his, trying to read the intent in his ice-gray eyes, what she saw sent warring emotions churning through her.

His gaze wasn't lewd or filled with lust. Instead, it was hot and stormy.

Just like the fortune-teller said. Amelia's heart leaped into her throat, making it hard for her to breathe. She was terrified, of course. But a part of her longed to look more deeply behind the storm clouds in his eyes, and find out what haunted him.

A muscle in his jaw ticked and his lips flattened, drawing her attention. His mouth was straight and wide. What would it be like to kiss this mysterious stranger?

Instantly his stormy eyes grew as cold as stone. He straightened. "Let's go. I want to meet your father."

"My—?" Dear heavens, he was after her dad. Terror slid like an ice cube down her spine.

Not for herself. Not now. *Now* she understood. He'd had plenty of chances to do whatever he wanted to her, if that was his plan.

Something far worse was going on. Something she couldn't even imagine. But she knew that he was connected to the pirate ships.

She didn't know what he planned to do once he got inside their house. She just knew she couldn't let him. She had to protect her dad.

She felt the familiar weight of her cell phone in her jeans' pocket. If she could somehow call Police Captain

Swanson without the stranger hearing her, maybe she could foil his plans.

But how?

She could feign nausea. If she stuck her finger down her throat, maybe she could dial the captain while the stranger thought she was puking.

Captain Swanson would see her number. He'd know there was something wrong.

Good. She had a plan.

The stranger's eyes flickered. He'd heard her sigh of relief. She clutched at her belly and moaned, but it was no use.

He reached out and with one spare motion, pulled her back against him and patted her down.

"Ah," he muttered. "Cell phone—and what's this?"

Amelia heard the sound of pills rattling. Her heart pounded. "Just vitamins."

"Vitamins?" The stranger held up the vial so it caught an anemic glow from the spotlights shining on the cliff house. "Vitamins for the heart? Reginald Hopkins. Your dad has a heart condition."

Amelia shook her head even as her stomach sank to the ground. No need to pretend nausea now. The real thing clenched her gut and filled her mouth with acrid saliva. "I've already told you what I can do for you. Leave my father alone."

"Sorry. Can't." He loosened his hold, but left his hot palm resting on the curve of her spine. She knew if she made a move, he'd be on her in a flash. "Now. Let's go inside and you can introduce me to your dad."

"What am I supposed to say to him?"

"Tell him the truth."

She glared at him as his eyes sparkled—with amusement or anticipation? "The truth. That presupposes that you've told me the truth."

"Tell him you've brought me home for the night."

His words hit their mark in her brain. Dear heavens, she'd underestimated him again. He'd just been biding his time.

"Is…is that the truth?"

He cocked his head to one side.

"But you promised—"

"Promised? I only promised you one thing." He touched her chin.

She cringed away and pushed at his hand. Why had she thought he'd promised not to hurt her? Was it just the way he'd looked at her?

"So that's it?" She swallowed, trying to stop the flutter in her throat. Her voice was already quivering. "You want me to sleep with you? And if I agree, what then? Will you go away?"

Her eyes stung and her throat felt raw. In fact, she felt raw all over, as if he'd flayed the skin off her bones. Could she do it? Could she lie with this stranger?

Hell yes, if it would keep her father safe. She frowned. "Well? Will you go away if I sleep with you?"

"I'm afraid not, Amelia." He drew out her name. *Ah-mee-lee-yah.* His eyes glittered in the darkness. "No matter how much fun you and I might have—it's your dad I'm after."

Chapter Three

Amelia's eyes grew huge and round. "No, please," she whispered. "What can you possibly want with my father? He's never hurt anyone in his life."

"That's true. He hasn't," Cole said, hardening his heart when he saw her shoulders slump in relief. "But that's not the issue."

Tears welled in her eyes. She blinked, and one spilled down her cheek. "Then what is?" she cried. "Tell me *something*. If I knew what you wanted, I could give it to you."

"You will. Now open the door."

She hesitated, then reached for the knob.

"Hold it." He wrapped his fingers around her upper arm. "Turn off the alarm."

She tried not to react, but her body language gave her away, and he could tell that she knew it.

"Don't waste my time, Amelia. We both know the alarm is on."

Two more tears slipped down her cheeks as she pressed on a rock to the left of the door. The "rock" slid aside, revealing a keypad.

Cole caught her hand. "If you do anything to alert anyone, I promise you it will be a *deadly* mistake. Do you understand?"

Her throat moved, and then she nodded.

It pained him to see her so defeated. Someday, once all this was over, he hoped he could tell her how brave she'd been today.

But right now, all of his concentration, all his strength, needed to be on the job at hand. It was his bad luck that the yacht-builder's daughter was so damned attractive. And her bad luck that both their lives depended on him playing his part to perfection.

As she pressed a sequence of numbers, he committed the code to memory. An almost silent click sounded and she reached for the doorknob again.

He put his hand over hers and felt the fine trembling that told him she was barely holding herself together. "Who's here?"

"My father. Our housekeeper, Mrs. Winston. That's it."

He squeezed her hand. "Who else?"

"S-sometimes a few of the guys will come up and play poker with Dad. But he's been—under the weather the past couple of days."

"His heart."

"Please…no one knows about his heart condition. Not even Mrs. Winston. My father is a very proud man. He's always been strong and smart. Always been able to do anything he set his mind to."

"I'm afraid that's about to change."

She squeezed her eyes shut and pressed her knuckles against her mouth. After a few seconds she spoke. "Are you going to kill us?"

"I hope it doesn't come to that."

"If I'm going to die, don't I deserve to know what I'm dying for?"

"You'll know soon enough." He let go of her hand. "Now, put on a happy face and go inside. Don't forget I'm right behind you."

As she turned the knob, she muttered a rude but apt description of him under her breath.

He agreed totally.

As she opened the door, he thought of something that had been niggling at the edge of his brain. "Wait a second. Is your dad's heart condition affecting his work? Is that why this season's yachts are throwbacks to past years?"

She turned, her expression carefully blank. "Why would you say that?"

"Because for the past three years I've been studying your dad's designs. It's pretty obvious." He let his gaze drift down her body and back up. When he met her gaze, she looked away.

"It's why you did that sexy photo shoot for this year's calendar, isn't it? To draw attention away from the yachts?"

Two spots of red in her cheeks told him he was right. "I don't get it. Wouldn't it have made more sense to underplay the calendar rather than make it the flashiest one in years?"

She lifted her chin. "Hopkins Yachts are never downplayed. *That* would have given it away."

They stepped into a stone foyer. Beyond, Cole saw a vast stretch of glass wall that looked out over Raven's Cliff's small harbor. In the center of the wall was a set of unsightly steel doors. *The elevator.*

That made sense now, too. Hopkins needed it to get up and down the cliff. It had been added after his heart attack.

Voices from the opposite side of the room stopped Cole. He slid his hand into his pocket and wrapped his fingers around his SIG-Sauer, hoping like hell he wouldn't have to use it.

He took Amelia's arm and pressed the barrel of the gun into her side. Startled, she jerked.

"Who's that?" he whispered in her ear. "And where are they?"

"That's Dad, but I don't know who's with him. His desk is to your right."

"Okay. Follow my lead. If you lose your cool, it's your dad who'll pay." He nudged her with the gun again.

She nodded and took a deep breath. With the gun barrel pressed against her side, he nudged her forward.

"Dad?"

"Amelia? Come here."

Amelia frowned. Her father sounded worried. "Dad? Is something wrong?"

Reginald Hopkins was sitting behind his desk in his pajamas and a maroon lounging robe. On the other side of the desk, in a yellow leather chair, sat Ross Fancher, assembly manager for Hopkins Boatworks.

Oh, no. Ross had the notion that he and she were dating. She'd been out to dinner with him a couple of times, but she'd carefully kept their friendship from moving to the next level.

Still, she'd rather not announce in front of him that she was taking a stranger to her suite for the night.

"Amelia—" Ross started, glaring at the man with her.

"Dad," she said quickly, hoping to cover the questions she was sure Ross was about to ask. "What are you doing up? Ross, I thought you'd know better than to keep Dad up so late. He's had that flu bug. What's going on?"

She shifted. Tension radiated from the stranger. She felt it across the distance that separated them. He'd taken the gun barrel away from her side, but she knew the weapon was in his pocket—and she knew he was capable of using it.

Ross stood. "Amelia—"

Amelia looked past him to her father. She put all the innocent pleading she could muster into her gaze. Her dad had always been a sucker for her big brown eyes. She prayed he'd understand her silent plea to get rid of Ross.

After a sharp look at her and the stranger, Reginald Hopkins cleared his throat. "Ross, why don't you run along? I am tired. I'll fill Amelia in on what's happening."

Ross glared over her head at the stranger. "Amelia, what's going on here. Who in h—"

"Ross!"

Amelia knew that tone. Her dad wasn't about to let Ross say another word.

Ross knew the tone, too. "Good night, Reg. 'Night Amelia." Ross sidestepped them and headed for the elevator.

Amelia felt the stranger turn. He was watching Ross to make sure he left.

Once the nearly silent doors shut and the swish that

announced the elevator's descent whispered through the air, Amelia felt the stranger relax. It was fascinating how she could feel what he was feeling, even across the inches separating them.

"Amelia?" Her father's voice was hoarse with exhaustion, but she knew him. He wouldn't budge until he found out why she'd come in after midnight with a stranger in tow. She'd never done that before—nothing like it.

She turned. "Dad, what's wrong?"

"Ross was telling me about the fleet of so-called pirate ships that docked at the harbor a little while ago. Apparently they sailed into the harbor like a scene from a movie. The pirates stormed the docks while the fireworks were going off. At first everybody thought it was part of the celebration. But they roughed up some people and apparently waved machine guns around. And now the mayor is missing."

"Mayor Wells—missing?" *What next?* "Oh, no. What happened?"

"Nobody seems to know." He looked at the man behind her. "Young man, who are you?"

Amelia turned. She'd like to hear the answer to that question herself.

"Mr. Hopkins, my name is Cole. I need some information from you."

"*My name is Cole* doesn't tell me anything. Who are you?" He shot the stranger a demanding glare. Without taking his eyes off him, he spoke to her.

"Amelia? Who is he?"

"She doesn't know," Cole said. "Is there anyone else in the house? Your housekeeper?"

Her dad's dark brows lowered. "Mrs. Winston lives down the hill, near the boatyard."

"That doesn't answer *my* question. Is she here?"

"No. She left around eleven."

"Is that elevator accessible from below?"

"Yes. Until it's turned off from up here. Mrs. Winston has a key. She locks it at night, unless we have a visitor, like tonight," Amelia replied. "I'll lock it now."

"No." Cole held up his hand. "Leave it alone." Glancing at his watch, he figured Chien Fou was on his way here with the mayor. The plan was for Cole to have the Hopkinses' house secured by 1:00 a.m. and to make sure the elevator was operational. It was after that now.

Amelia's face turned pale. "You're waiting for someone."

Her gaze snapped to his pocket, where his weapon bulged, and understanding filled her eyes with new horror. "Oh, dear heavens, you're one of those pirates."

Cole winced inwardly at the horror and disgust in her expression. *Just wait,* he thought bitterly. *You ain't seen nothing yet.*

"One of the pirates?" Hopkins repeated, his tone sharp. "Amelia, why did you bring him here?"

"She had no choice, sir," Cole responded. "I kidnapped her."

"My God, sugar, are you all right?"

Amelia stepped in front of her father. "Let my dad go to bed." Her eyes blazed like amber in her pale face.

Cole studied her. Her love and worry for her father radiated from her like heat. How would it feel to have someone care that much? To be that fiercely protective?

Cole thought about his own father. Maybe the old man had cared for him once—a long time ago, before his greed and self-indulgence had turned him into a traitor.

Shame washed over him, familiar, yet still raw. His father's betrayal had changed Cole, and he knew it. When he'd graduated with a Ph.D. in Political Science, he'd felt as if he was on top of the world. He'd been looking forward to following in his dad's footsteps.

Now, if he were honest with himself, and that didn't happen often these days, he'd have to admit that during the three years he'd been working under deep cover, infiltrating the Global Freedom Front, he'd come to the conclusion that he didn't really expect to get out of this assignment alive.

Only during the past two days had these other thoughts occurred to him. Only since he'd first seen Amelia and reflected on what he'd signed up to do had he wondered if he was as uninterested in life as he'd convinced himself he was.

Amelia's chin went up and she turned toward the elevator. Her movement brought his thoughts back to the job at hand and he heard what she'd already heard— the quiet hum of the elevator's motor.

His pulse thrummed as the door slid open.

Amelia shot him a look from over her shoulder. Her expression pierced him like a poisoned arrow. She backed up, her arms spread defensively.

She was making sure she was between the elevator door and her father.

Cole took his weapon out of his jacket pocket. He should be holding his hostages at gunpoint.

He steeled himself against the urge to copy Amelia's actions—to put himself in front of her and her father as the leader of the notorious and deadly Global Freedom Front stepped out of the elevator.

Behind him stood his three most trusted guards, each carrying a MAC-10 machine pistol. Chien Fou's hands were empty.

During the past three years, Cole had developed a deep knowledge and understanding of the man the world and his followers knew only as Chien Fou, or *Mad Dog*. He'd made it his business to understand the terrorist leader's motivation—his passion. It was the only way he'd stayed alive this long.

The American, who had put himself in power as the leader of the deadliest terrorist group operating inside the United States, only cared about three things: the demise of the American government, the game of chess and himself.

"Amelia, Mr. Hopkins, this is Chien Fou."

The name sent shock skittering along Amelia's nerve endings. *Chien Fou*. She did her best to keep her expression neutral as the full truth of their situation dawned on her.

She, along with everyone else who listened to national news, knew Chien Fou's name. She was looking at one of the most notorious terrorists on the planet, the leader of the infamous domestic fringe group, the Global Freedom Front. And she, her dad and the town of Raven's Cliff were in his clutches.

No one had been able to identify him, but rumor had it that he was an American—a traitor to his country and the cause of freedom.

After the Global Freedom Front's first attack, the media had plastered an artist's sketch created from a witness's description all over newspapers, TV and the Internet. The sketch had become as famous as the drawing of the Unabomber. It depicted a broad-faced man with a plaid scarf wrapped around his neck and a Fedora pulled down over his forehead. The shaded eyes in the sketch hinted at Asian features.

Tonight, he wasn't wearing the scarf or the hat. The implication chilled her to the bone. The fact that this notorious terrorist was here without a disguise meant that he didn't care if they could identify him. And there was only one reason he wouldn't care.

He planned to kill them.

Amelia's pulse kicked into high gear. Thoughts chased each other around in her brain until she was sure she was going crazy.

Terrorists had taken over Raven's Cliff. The man the fortune-teller had told her to see with her heart, not her mind, was a traitor to his country. She, her father and everyone in Raven's Cliff were going to die, and it was all her fault.

If she'd tried harder... If she hadn't been so scared... If—

Amelia squeezed her eyes shut, trying to chase off the whirling thoughts. When she opened them, another shock awaited her.

Behind Chien Fou, Mayor Wells stumbled out of the elevator. His hands were cuffed in front of him and his face was pale and dripping with sweat.

Three armed men followed him. A fourth stayed in the elevator. As the door slid shut, two of the guards moved to opposite sides of the room. The third kept his gun barrel stuck in the mayor's back.

Amelia retreated another step. She needed to get to her father, to make sure he was all right.

"Cole, why aren't the prisoners tied up?" Chien Fou smiled at Cole.

Amelia had never seen anything more sinister, more chilling, than Chien Fou's smile.

"There was a visitor here when I got here, Leader."

Amelia was shocked by the obsequious tone in Cole's voice. He wasn't the type to bow to another. As she'd thought before, he was the captain—not the crew.

"Who?" Chien Fou snapped.

Cole looked at Amelia, his sharp eyes signaling a warning.

"Ross Fancher," she said.

"Yes?"

How did everything the terrorist leader said sound like a threat? She lifted her chin and gave him a steady look.

For some reason, he found that amusing. He chuckled. "What is Ross Fancher to you or your father?"

"He's assembly-line manager. He supervises the building of the boats. He just left a few minutes ago."

"Assembly-line manager. Interesting. Then it is fortunate that his injury has not proven fatal."

Alarm streaked through her like lightning. "Injury? Is he all right? We need to call a doctor."

Before she knew it the guard on the south side of the room was at her side, pushing the long barrel of his gun into her flesh just beneath her breast. He was shorter than her, and already heaving with exertion. His breath smelled like stale tobacco and beer.

"I can assure you that your friend will be all right. In fact, he will be helpful to us in carrying out our plan," Chien Fou said. "I suggest that you stay calm, Miss Hopkins."

"Stay calm?" She flinched as the gun barrel sank more deeply into her flesh. "You've taken us hostage. You've hurt people. Forgive me if I'm finding it a little hard to *stay calm* right now."

"Then we'll have to find a way to help you."

"Leader." Cole spoke calmly. "Maybe we should get settled for the night. There's not much of it left, and we've got some hard work ahead of us."

"Always the level head, Cole." Chien Fou nodded. "Abel, you—"

Wood scraped against wood. Before Amelia could react, her father said, "Don't move." He stood behind his desk, his face pale, his expression a mixture of fear and determination. He gripped a semiautomatic pistol in his unsteady hands.

"Dad, no!"

Suddenly three deadly looking machine pistols were aimed at her dad's chest.

At the same time, Cole vaulted toward her father. He grabbed the gun and wrenched it away. Her dad gasped for breath. Cole pushed him down into his chair.

Her dad's arrhythmia medicine. Cole still had it, and it was way past time for his bedtime dose.

"Please." She let all her fear and worry show in her voice. "My father is just getting over the flu," she said. "He needs his *anti-flu* medication. And he needs to rest."

Chien Fou gestured to the guard whose gun barrel was back in Amelia's side. "Get his medicine. Bring it to me."

No. Just what she hoped wouldn't happen. If Chien Fou saw her dad's prescription bottle, he'd know he had a heart condition. She knew with intuitive certainty that the terrorist leader would have no patience with infirmity. She glanced desperately at Cole.

Cole's gaze slipped past her as he dug into his pocket. "Here it is. I took it when I took her cell phone." He held it up between thumb and forefinger.

For a second Chien Fou hesitated and a frown creased his forehead. Then he nodded. "Good. You hold on to it. If he needs it, give him one—just one."

"He needs it now," Amelia insisted.

"Yes, Leader." Cole shook a tablet into his palm and handed it to her dad, who picked up a water glass sitting on his desk and quickly downed the pill.

"Now, if there are no more illnesses to treat…" Chien Fou rubbed his hands together. "We need arrangements for the night. I'm ready to retire. Where shall we all sleep?"

"There are—" Amelia's throat fluttered with apprehension "—seven bedrooms. My father's suite is there." She nodded at a door beyond his office. "My rooms are on the opposite wall, beyond the stairs. There is another master suite upstairs, plus two smaller bedrooms. And a small room with its own bath behind the kitchen."

"Abel, you take the mayor and Mr. Hopkins to his suite. Handcuff Hopkins. Search the suite to be sure Mr. Hopkins has no more weapons. It would be regrettable if we had to use force to convince him not to play the hero."

Amelia stiffened. "Dad, please. Just do what they say."

"I'd be a whole lot more cooperative if I knew what's going on here."

"Dad—"

The guard named Abel produced a pair of handcuffs and quickly cuffed her dad, then dragged the mayor over next to him.

"Cole," Chien Fou said, "I want you out here, keeping an eye on everything."

"Ha," the guard at Amelia's side shouted. "That means I get to spend the night guarding the beautiful girl." He touched her hair with one hand. "We will have fun, eh?"

Amelia recoiled.

Cole didn't move, although every muscle in his body tensed in response to Habib's implication. He had to protect Amelia.

"Leader," Cole said, working to keep the desperation out of his voice. "I got us into the house. You know I have not asked for favors. But do I not deserve the woman? She is well-versed in her father's business. She will be an asset to our cause. We cannot afford to have her damaged." He shot Habib a glare. "And we all know how *enthusiastic* Habib is."

Amelia turned her haunted honey-colored eyes to his. Her abject terror made his chest ache. She didn't consider him any better than Habib, and he couldn't blame her.

Maybe once they were alone, he could prove to her that he didn't mean her any harm. *If* he could convince Chien Fou to let him guard her, and if the terrorist leader wasn't in one of his perverse moods.

Chien Fou's coal-black eyes studied Amelia, and a chill slithered down Cole's spine. He'd never seen Chien Fou express any interest in a woman. It hadn't occurred to him that the man might want Amelia for himself.

Cole shifted cautiously onto the balls of his feet. He still held his SIG. If Chien Fou allowed Habib to have her, or took her for himself, Cole would have to stop him.

There were some things he wouldn't do—not even if it meant his three years under cover infiltrating the Global Freedom Front would be wasted.

Not even if it meant his death.

Your two worlds are about to collide and your young woman may be crushed in the collision.

The fortune-teller's words echoed in his ears and a faint memory of spice and roses tickled his nostrils. He shook off the distracting sense that the woman was nearby.

Chien Fou met Cole's gaze and for an instant, their wills locked in a silent battle.

Cole slipped his finger into the trigger guard on his SIG.

Then Chien Fou smiled. "Take her, Cole. You've earned the right."

He had to force himself not to slump in relief. He heard a shaky sigh from Amelia and a curse from Habib.

"You sons of bitches!" Hopkins blurted, yanking away from Abel. "Keep your filthy hands off my daughter!"

Abel backhanded the older man with his fist.

He fell.

"Dad!" Amelia lunged forward. Cole had to grab her by the waist to stop her from throwing herself at Abel.

"Stop it—" he hissed, pinning her to his side with one arm. "Leader. We can't afford to have Hopkins injured."

"Abel. Mr. Hopkins is understandably upset," Chien Fou said evenly. "We are guests in his home. If you do not remember how to accept hospitality, I can call another guard and send you back to the ships."

Chien Fou's voice was soft and amicable, his words reasonable, but Abel turned a sickly shade of green. "Yes, Leader." He reached out to help Hopkins up. "Pardon, sir, I apologize for lifting my hand to you."

"Now, since we all understand our roles here, please escort the mayor and Mr. Hopkins to his suite for the night."

"I'm not budging," Hopkins insisted, gingerly touching his jaw where the skin was turning dark red, "until you give me an explanation for this. Why have you invaded my house?"

"Mr. Hopkins, of course. Let me apologize. You don't know who I am, do you?" Without waiting for an answer, Chien Fou went on. "I am called Chien Fou, and my organization, the Global Freedom Front, is destroying the economic stranglehold the United States has on the rest of the world."

"You're nothing but a filthy terrorist." Hopkins coughed.

Chien Fou laughed. "Ah, but, sir, one country's terrorist is another country's liberator."

"So what do you want with me and my family?"

"With your help, we will transform a fleet of your yachts into floating bombs."

"Floating—" Amelia choked out.

"Floating bombs?" Hopkins repeated. "What in the devil's name are you talking about?"

"We will blow up a fleet of oil tankers off the East

Coast. In doing so we will accomplish what no one else
has ever done. Using your luxury yachts as weapons,
we will destroy the U.S. economy."

Chapter Four

An hour later, after Chien Fou and his guards had been shown to their rooms, the gray-eyed stranger who'd brought the terrorists to her home took Amelia's arm and led her into her suite. Amelia wanted to scream and run, but she had nowhere to go and no one but the enemy to hear her cries.

And she was her father's only protection.

Cole closed the double doors and surveyed her rooms. With a shake of his head and a harsh laugh, he turned those gray eyes on her. "Tough job, being a rich heiress."

"You don't know anything about me," Amelia said, horrified when her voice broke. She lifted her chin and looked him in the eye, doing her best not to falter beneath his icy glare.

He was unfazed by her puny effort at bravery.

Unfortunately, she couldn't say the same. She was definitely intimidated by him. She turned away. "I have to…" She gestured toward her bathroom.

He stalked over and pushed open the sliding mirrors that divided it from the rest of her suite. "Not until I check it out first."

He stopped and turned. "After you, of course."

Fear clutched at her throat as she walked past him. He was so tall, so—dominant. He made her luxurious suite seem small.

But then, the whole house seemed tiny, now that it was filled with dangerous, murderous men.

Chien Fou was in the luxurious guest suite right above hers. His guards had staked out the other bedrooms. All except Abel and Habib, who were sharing guard duty in front of her father's suite.

Her father. He'd looked so fragile as the men had handcuffed him and led him away. She'd been at his side constantly since his heart attack, protecting him—from the stress of running a multimillion-dollar boat-building company, from curious friends who kept asking about his health, from anything that might trigger a second attack.

"I want to check on my father," she said, crossing her arms as she faced Cole.

He was scanning every inch of the bath, and she was sure not one thing escaped his attention. Certainly not the telephone.

"You're not leaving here until morning," he said over his shoulder.

"It's already morning."

That earned her a narrow, sideways look. "Don't screw with me, Amelia. I'm tired, you're annoying and tomorrow's going to be a long day."

Beneath her fear, a coal of anger caught and flared. "Oh, please forgive me. Of course you're tired. You've been so busy bullying a woman half your size and terrorizing a sick man. You *must* be exhausted."

"Don't flatter yourself." He raked her with his gaze. "I might tip two-ten soaking wet. You haven't weighed one-oh-five since you were…what, twelve?"

"Are you going to let me check on my dad?"

Cole didn't even bother answering. He reached past her and picked up the telephone handset. "Is this a separate line?"

Amelia gave as good as she got. No answer for him, either.

"Don't ever play poker, Amelia. You don't have the face for it."

"It's a safety feature, in case the house is taken over by filthy traitors."

For an instant a shadow darkened his gaze. "You're a laugh a minute, Amelia."

"Would you stop calling me that? My name is Amelia—Ah-melya, not Ah-mee-*lee*-yah." She lifted her chin and glared at him. "Now if you're satisfied that I don't have a secret arsenal in here, I could use some privacy."

Still holding the telephone handset, Cole stepped backward. "Be my guest. You have five minutes. If you're not out, I'm coming in after you."

He left, sliding the mirrored doors closed.

Amelia sat on her vanity bench and put her head in her hands. For a moment, her tight hold on control melted and the horror of their situation slithered through her, setting her whole body to trembling. Tears stung her eyes. She wrapped her arms around herself and rocked back and forth, holding her breath, trying not to sob.

Three sharp raps on the door echoed through her like gunshots.

"Just—*wait*—a minute," she snapped. She stood and turned on the cold water faucet. Holding her wrists under the tap, she let water cool her wrists until her hands stopped trembling, then she splashed her face.

Cole rapped on the door again.

"Wait!" She grabbed the fleece pajamas hanging behind the door and quickly changed, then took a deep breath and slid the door open.

Cole's brows shot up when he saw her and his eyes scrutinized every inch of her.

She lifted her chin. "Like them? Sorry I don't have any in your size."

"I'm not planning to sleep."

What did he mean by that? She studied his face, but his expression didn't tell her anything. She crossed her arms and took a deep breath, sucking courage into her lungs. She closed her eyes briefly before speaking.

"If you're planning to rape me, could we get it over with? I'm very tired, and I have a feeling I'm going to need all the sleep I can get."

He moved.

Before she could react, he was right in front of her. He wrapped his fingers around her upper arm and got in her face. "You need to drop the attitude, Amelia. It's going to get you hurt. Very hurt. The Leader is not a fan of sarcasm."

Amelia stood there helplessly, feeling the strength of his hand, knowing he was right. Knowing how deadly these people were. But her only weapon was her wit and her tongue. If she stopped throwing barbs and sarcastic comments, she might as well give up.

"Well, I'm not a fan of terrorists." She jerked away from his grip and rubbed her arm.

Cole itched to shake some sense into that hard head of hers. Chien Fou had been in a good mood tonight, probably because his pirate-ship plan had worked. His men had pretended to be sailors on leave. In truth, they'd surrounded and seized control of the town, effectively putting a stranglehold on the residents.

As Cole well knew, Chien Fou's mood could change in a heartbeat. Tomorrow, the leader of the Global Freedom Front might not be so amicable. Cole had seen it happen. One day, the Leader had been idly discussing food with one of his employees, until the employee expressed a dislike for Chien Fou's favorite brand of hot sauce. He'd shot him.

"You'd better watch your mouth, Amelia, or you're going to regret it. Even if you aren't worried about yourself, think of your father."

He stood with his back against the wall and his hand resting on the butt of his gun as he watched Amelia turn back the covers on her bed and climb in.

She obviously had no idea how incredibly sexy she looked in her pink fleece pajamas, with her bare toes sticking out. She'd twisted her hair up somehow. It left her neck bare, except for a few strands of honey-brown that appeared to caress her vulnerable nape like the fingers of a lover.

Cole shifted. *Think about baseball—or what you're putting her through.*

But the part of his brain that ruled his libido wasn't listening.

He wanted her. He'd wanted her from the moment

he'd opened that calendar and seen her full, painted lips and her slender yet curvy body. Before he'd realized who she was.

Under the covers, she looked small and vulnerable. And scared. She was still afraid he might attack her. And he knew he hadn't done one thing to reassure her. He couldn't.

She *had* to remain terrified of him. Her safety—her very life depended on it. If she had any clue of his real plans, she wouldn't be able to hide it. Her face, her actions, would give her away.

"Cole? Are you going to stay over there?"

Her tentative question tore through him raggedly, like a dull knife through cloth. "Yeah. Don't worry. I was serious when I told the Leader we can't afford to have you damaged. We have bigger plans for you than to be a plaything for a bunch of horny thugs."

Her breath escaped in a sigh of relief and she sank deeper into the covers. All he could see was her dark hair.

Rest now, Ah-mee-lee-yah. She'd need all the strength she could muster for what was to come.

After a few seconds she stirred. "Chien Fou said *floating bombs,* what did he mean?"

A dull whirring began, and Cole felt the floor vibrate beneath his heavy boots.

She shot up in bed. Her eyes glistened in the dim light.

"What's that?" he demanded.

"The elevator."

"Stay here." He drew his gun and slipped out the door.

Amelia pulled the covers up to her chin as Cole rushed out. She felt the vibrations stop.

Who was on the elevator? More terrorists? Mrs. Winston?

She checked the clock on her nightstand. Three o'clock in the morning. Their housekeeper wasn't due until seven. She'd have a stroke when she saw the horde of rough men who'd taken over the house.

The faint sound of voices—harsh, agitated voices— carried through the walls. Who were they? And what were they doing? Arguing? Fighting?

Amelia had to know what was going on.

Okay she didn't *have* to, but her only other choice was to cower in bed like a hysterical female. And she'd never cowered in her life. She wasn't about to start now.

She jumped out of bed and stepped over to the wall that separated her suite from the front room. No matter how hard she tried, she couldn't make out what the voices were saying. But she could tell by their tone that something was wrong.

If she were in her father's study, she could unlock the cabinets that lined the exterior wall and watch what was going on via the security monitors. All the rooms in the house and the entrances and exits to the offices at the bottom of the elevator were monitored.

Frustration burned through her. She hated not being in control. Hated it so much that she'd spent her entire life making sure she never let herself get into a situation where she wasn't.

The last time she could remember feeling like this was the night of her dad's heart attack. That night she'd felt totally helpless.

She wasn't about to let anyone make her feel that way again. Certainly not these thugs.

Besides, they were plotting against the United States. She had a patriotic duty to do everything she could to stop them.

She crossed the room and put her hand on the door handle, ready to ease it open and sneak out into the hall so she could hear what was going on.

But all at once, the handle was jerked out of her hand.

She recoiled with a cry.

The door slammed against the wall and a bulky figure blocked the light from the hall. It was Habib, the guard with the bad teeth.

Alarm jangled through her nerves. "What are you doing? Get out of here," she commanded.

"So he left you alone, eh? Cole's not a very smart boy." Habib advanced.

Amelia took another step backward. She ran through a split-second mental inventory of her suite—what could she use as a weapon?

"That's okay. You and me, we'll have a good time." Habib's mouth widened in an ugly, threatening grin.

"No! Get out. I'll scream!"

The banker's lamp, on her writing table. Its brass base was heavy. If she could get her hands on it, maybe she could knock Habib out.

She stepped sideways, inching carefully toward the table.

Habib lunged. Amelia dodged. Her hip slammed into the corner of the table. Crying out in pain, she went down.

The terrorist stood over her, triumph and lust distorting his face.

She was trapped. There was nothing within reach.

No way to help herself. *Where was Cole?* She opened her mouth to scream for help.

Habib grabbed a handful of her hair and jerked her up.

Pain seared her scalp. Her scream died in her throat. She flailed her arms and legs, trying to scratch, hit, kick—anything to stop him.

He clamped a dirty hand over her mouth and slammed her bodily down onto her bed. His heavy body pinned hers.

Panicked, her eyes awash with tears of pain, Amelia curled her fingers and clawed at any exposed flesh she could reach—his hands, his neck, his face.

She connected and dug in.

With a startled grunt of pain, he pulled away and backhanded her.

The blow jarred her brain. She tried to squirm free, but he grabbed her wrists and wrenched her arms over her head.

Her heart thumped so fast and hard she couldn't catch a breath. Sick dread paralyzed her as his weight crushed her.

His heaving breaths sawed in her ears. His broad sweaty face filled her vision.

"No!" she cried weakly, lungs screaming for air. She pushed against his unbearable weight with all her might. But nothing worked. He was still on her, still crushing her. His thick, clammy fingers pawed at her pajama bottoms.

Then he was gone.

Amelia dug her heels into the mattress and pushed herself backward across the bed until she hit the head-board. She curled up into a ball, sobbing.

Cole burned with rage. He threw Habib across the room and lunged after him. Fisting his hand in the bastard's shirt, he lifted him bodily and slammed his fist into his face—once, twice, three times.

Habib's blood coated his fingers. He drew back his arm again. "You won't be able to hurt a woman when I'm done," he growled.

"Cole."

The quiet voice pierced his consciousness like a lance. *Chien Fou.*

It took a huge effort to loosen his fist and let go of Habib. The disgusting piece of crap crawled out of his reach, grunting and whimpering.

"What's going on?" Chien Fou stood quietly, as he always did. His personal bodyguard stood at attention beside him, holding a MAC-10 machine pistol.

Cole rounded on the Leader. "Isn't it obvious?" he growled.

Chien Fou held up a hand. "It's over now. Watch your tone."

Cole bit the inside of his cheek and took a long ragged breath. "Yes, Leader."

There was nothing Cole wanted more than to finish beating Habib to a bloody pulp. But as his rage dissipated, he saw in Chien Fou's face that Amelia's attacker would no longer be a problem.

Nausea churned in his gut. The terrorist leader had an efficient method for dispatching problems.

"Leader—"

"As you said earlier," Chien Fou interrupted, "we cannot afford to have Miss Hopkins damaged. Especially now. Comfort her. Reassure her. Whatever it takes. Just do not let this incident interfere with our goal."

Cole nodded, flexing his fingers. His hand ached from pummeling Habib.

The disgusting man cowered on the floor, spitting blood and whimpering.

Chien Fou's head inclined slightly. His bodyguard immediately stepped over, nudged Habib with his machine pistol and gruffly ordered him to stand.

"We will meet at ten o'clock in the morning," Chien Fou said to Cole. "It promises to be another long day."

He left. Behind him, his bodyguard marched Habib out at gunpoint. Habib's whimpering had degenerated into quiet moans. He knew his fate was sealed.

Cole locked the double doors behind them, then turned to Amelia. She was curled in on herself, her knees up, her head bent. Her tangled brown hair hid her face. She was trembling, and every so often he could hear a small sob.

The terrorist leader's voice echoed in his ears. *Comfort her. Reassure her. Whatever it takes.*

Perversely, that was exactly what Cole wanted to do. He wanted nothing more than to be able to give her some reassurance that he would take care of her.

But that wasn't his assignment. He was tasked with protecting America from terrorists. The fate of a single life had to be weighed against the fate of millions.

Forcing his thoughts back to why he was here, he thought about the tiny cameras mounted discreetly above the crown molding in each room and the wall of polished cherrywood cabinets in Hopkins's office. He'd bet money that they hid a bank of monitors. Smart for

Hopkins's security—damned inconvenient for Cole's purposes. He'd have to find out from Amelia where each and every camera was, before Chien Fou discovered them.

Meanwhile, he had to play his part in this grim charade.

Amelia wiped tears from her cheeks.

Damn it. Cole knew her attack was his fault. He should never have left her. Someone else could have investigated who'd ridden up in the elevator. Someone else could have been first on the scene.

But Cole had been afraid it was one of Hopkins's employees or the housekeeper Amelia had mentioned. He hadn't wanted to risk another innocent person's life.

Walking quietly over to the opposite side of the bed, he spoke gently. "Amelia?"

She started then tightened her arms around her knees.

"Amelia, it's over now."

She made a small, distressed noise.

Against his better judgment, Cole reached out a hand and touched a strand of her hair. "I'm sorry," he whispered.

She didn't move.

"Can I—"

"Can you what?" she muttered, her voice muffled.

"I just—"

She jerked her head up. Her eyes were wide and haunted, half hidden by tangled waves. "Can you what? Kidnap me? Manhandle me? Invade my home? Endanger my father's life? Let a filthy terrorist paw me?" She vaulted up and pushed past him.

To a safe distance, he noticed.

"What else can you possibly do? Are you going to take your turn now?"

"Amelia, calm down. It's over. You're safe."

"Safe?" She laughed as tears welled in her eyes and spilled down her cheeks. She swiped at them angrily. "Safe?

"My room was invaded by a madman who wanted to rape me. My house is filled with people plotting to destroy America. My town is hostage to terrorists. Is that what you call *safe?*"

Cole didn't know what to say. She was right. He had nothing to offer her but empty words. So he told her the only truth he knew. "Habib will never bother you again."

Amelia stared at him, openmouthed. "You're lying. You can't guarantee that." She shuddered. "He's out there…waiting. Next time—" Her voice rose, headed toward hysteria.

Cole clenched his jaw. "No. There will never be a next time."

She wiped both hands over her face. "How can you promise…?" She paused, staring at him. After a few seconds, her face drained of color and she swayed.

He took a step toward her, but she held up a hand. "He wouldn't," she whispered.

Cole just nodded.

"Oh, dear heavens." This time when she swayed, she didn't right herself.

Cole dove toward her and caught her just before her legs collapsed completely.

"No!" She squirmed and fought. "No! Don't touch me."

Fearful of hurting her, Cole let go. "You're about to faint. You need to lie down. Let me help."

She shook her head vehemently. "You've got blood on your hands. You're a filthy terrorist, just like Habib. Don't ever touch me again." Wrapping her arms around herself and hunching her shoulders, she inched toward the bathroom. "I'm going to take a bath."

Cole nodded. "That's a good idea."

Just as she started to close the bathroom door, he stopped her.

The look she gave him was at once terrified and defiant. He felt like dirt under her feet.

"Give me the keys to your suite."

She gaped at him. "Wha—"

"The keys, Amelia. I won't leave you vulnerable to an attack again. I'll lock you in."

Her chin lifted, although it trembled. "And you won't risk me locking *you* out."

He inclined his head.

"I won't give them to you."

Cole sighed. "Fine. I'll find them."

Her gaze flickered to a spot behind him. *Gotcha,* he thought.

He backed away from the door.

"Cole?"

He glanced at her sidelong.

"Chien Fou wouldn't really kill Habib—"

Her question was interrupted by the unmistakable rat-tat-tat of a machine pistol.

Chapter Five

Cole pocketed the ring of keys he'd found in the drawer of Amelia's writing desk. He'd already tried them in the suite door and pulled matching keys off the ring in her purse. As soon as he could manage it without being seen, he'd try them in the locks of the rest of the house.

Behind him the door to her bathroom opened. He turned.

Soft light, diffused by the steam from her bath, seemed to swirl around Amelia. She was so beautiful and ethereal that she made his throat ache.

She'd pulled her damp hair back into a ponytail. The jeans and long-sleeved T-shirt she wore looked casual, but Cole figured that kind of casual didn't come cheap.

Then he noticed her feet. She was barefoot. Pink-tipped toes peeked out from the denim pant legs. With an effort, he dragged his eyes away from her sexy toes and met her gaze.

She'd been crying. That giant fist squeezed his heart.

Crap. If he didn't squelch this urge to be her own personal knight in shining armor, he was going to compromise the mission.

"You need to grab a couple of hours of sleep," he said gruffly. "You're going to need it."

She sniffed. "Sleep? How do you think I'm supposed to sleep? Terrorists have invaded my home. A man was murdered in my living room." She gestured shakily toward the north wall of her suite.

Cole pushed his fingers through his hair, then wiped his face. "There'll be a lot more of that if you don't cooperate. With Fancher dead, you're going to become—"

"Ross? Dead?" Her choked voice ripped through him.

Son of a— What was the matter with him, letting something like that slip?

Her eyes glazed over and her creamy skin faded to a sickly gray. The corners of her lips went white. "I thought Chien Fou said he was all right—"

Amelia's knees turned to water. She sank down onto the corner of her bed and clapped a hand over her mouth. "I'm going to be sick." She wasn't lying. Nausea churned in her stomach. The coffee she'd drunk—had it only been a few hours ago?—tried to crawl up her throat.

Ross, dead? She'd just seen him a few hours ago. He'd been her friend and a valuable asset to Hopkins's designs.

"Amelia, I'm sorry." Cole's face was shadowed with concern. "I wasn't thinking. I didn't mean to blurt it out like that."

"That's why someone came up in the elevator? To tell you Ross had died? Oh, dear heavens. What kind of nightmare is this? What are you people doing?"

"You know all you need to know."

"I don't know anything. I feel as if I'm in some bizarre dream. You're an American." She could hear her voice rising in pitch. Soon she'd be hysterical. Her hand fluttered to her throat.

"How can you support ruining the U.S. economy? What happened to your patriotism?"

He winced, an expression so fleeting that she could have misread it.

"You shouldn't waste your energy being self-righteous," he retorted. "You're going to need all you can muster. Now sleep or don't, I don't care, but whatever you do, keep your mouth shut. Trust me, you do *not* want to disturb the Leader."

"I can't sleep. Please, I need to see my father. He should hear about Ross from me. And Joey, Ross's brother. I have to tell Joey."

"Amelia, calm down. It's 4:00 a.m."

She wiped her eyes and looked at her watch. Only four o'clock in the morning? She felt years older since she'd run into this stranger on the street last night.

"I have to go see Joey. Ross was his only family."

"I'll go with you. I can explain about the accident."

"Accident?" Anger heated Amelia's cheeks. *"Accident?* You're going to tell Joey his brother died in an *accident?"*

"It *was* an accident. Fancher tried to rush one of the guards and the guard hit him with the butt of his rifle. Unfortunately when he fell, he hit his head on a cleat on one of the boats. They had the ship's doctor work on him, but it was no use."

"Oh." She pressed her fingertips against her mouth as her eyes stung with tears. "Poor Ross. I can't believe it. Dad will be devastated. Ross was just like a son to him."

"Like a son. That tick you off?"

"Tick me off? What are you talking about? Of course not. I know Dad wants—wanted Ross to take over the boatyard. But I'll be doing the designing. Dad hoped—" A stab of sadness caught her just under her breastbone. "Dad hoped Ross and I would—" She stopped again.

She shook her head. Why was she telling this stranger, this *traitor,* things about her personal life?

"Would what? Get married? That'd be convenient, wouldn't it?"

She stood and leveled a gaze at him. "I suppose it would. But since a boatload of filthy traitors murdered Ross, I guess it won't happen now." Her voice cracked on Ross's name.

Cole's mouth flattened and his jaw twitched. Had she made him angry? She hoped so. "What? Don't you like being called a traitor? I suppose you believe what your *leader* said. That one person's traitor is another's liberator?"

He dropped his gaze.

"Tell me, Cole, how did you and your fellow *liberators* decide on Raven's Cliff?"

Cole crossed his arms and leaned a shoulder against the corner of the archway that defined the entry to her suite. "It wasn't hard," he said. "Sleepy little town like Raven's Cliff. Tucked into the cliffs, easy to miss along the coastline. Nothing ever happens in a place like this. Nobody's thinking about danger."

Amelia felt like snorting in disgust. "That just goes to show what you know. You obviously didn't do your homework very well. You have no idea what's been going on here. Of all the towns along the Eastern Seaboard that you could have picked, why Raven's Cliff? Why now?"

"What are you talking about, why now?"

"The people of Raven's Cliff have gone through so much already, these past months. The Seaside Strangler, the poisoned fish, so much death and sadness. And now you storm the town and take hostages and…and kill people. Who else have you killed?"

Amelia thought of something. Cole had taken her cell phone, and she was certain they'd taken her dad's, but there was no way this band of marauders could gather up every single cell phone in Raven's Cliff. Even if no one had realized the danger yet, someone would— and then they'd call for help.

"It's only a matter of time—" She cut herself off and bit her lip.

Cole shot her a glance. "A matter of time? I know what you're thinking. Someone's bound to get suspicious. Well, think about this. It's your job to prepare a story for your workers that's so good it will keep them working and ensure that nobody will even think there's any need to call for help. You'll be talking to them at ten o'clock."

"You want *me* to come up with a plausible story? Fine. How about this? Terrorists have taken over the town and killed people. If you don't do as they say, they'll kill each of you and your families, too."

"I was thinking more along the lines of a top-secret government plot—so secret that if anyone mentions anything, even to their own family, terrorists could get wind of it and blow up the entire town to stop it."

Amelia uttered a short, sharp laugh. "Are you serious? Nobody's going to believe a secret government plot. It's way too farfetched."

Cole raised his brows. "You'd be surprised. Now be a good girl and think about what you're going to say. And if you're smart at all, you'll take my advice and grab some sleep."

"No thanks." Amelia shook her head. "Kind of hard to close my eyes while there's a traitor in my room."

Cole saw the hatred and disgust shining in her eyes. *Give me time,* he thought. *You'll hate me even more.* "By the way, I'm locking you in." He held up her key ring and shook it.

Amelia started, then looked over her shoulder toward her desk.

"If you have any more keys, you'd better give them to me now. Because I'll find them, even if I have to search you."

"You wouldn't dare."

"Try me."

Her eyes filled with alarm and he had to stop himself from taking her hand and swearing he'd never hurt her.

Damn it, from the first moment he'd laid eyes on Amelia three days ago, he'd struggled with his conscience. What had happened to his unflappable cool?

During the three years he'd been under deep cover with the Global Freedom Front, he'd witnessed some horrible things. Habib wasn't the first GFF member Chien Fou had executed because he'd displeased him. And the people of Raven's Cliff weren't the first innocent civilians who'd been placed in danger by Chien Fou's single-minded mission to destroy the U.S. economy.

But this *was* the first time Cole had been unable to see past the individual and focus on the big picture.

He *had* to harden his heart toward Amelia. Chien Fou could smell weakness a mile away, and he never hesitated to attack. That could mean Amelia's death.

Without looking at her, he turned and left, locking the doors behind him. In the living room, he encountered Abel, who was nodding over his machine pistol.

"Hey, I can take over down here if you want me to. I can't sleep."

Abel jerked upright. "You mean, your *hostage* did not wear you out?"

Cole's scalp burned with quick anger. "Watch what you say."

Abel shrugged. "The Leader won't like it."

"He'll okay it for me. Anything going on?"

Abel shook his head. "Nothing. Did you hear that the Leader's bodyguard shot Habib?"

Cole nodded. "Bastard attacked Ms. Hopkins after the Leader warned him against it. Harsh punishment, but no less than he deserved."

"I will go into the room off the kitchen and nap, if you're sure you don't mind. Wake me before the Leader comes downstairs."

"He said ten o'clock. He won't show up a minute before, as long as nothing happens. You know how he is about his sleep."

As soon as Abel disappeared into the small bedroom next to the kitchen, Cole scoped out the large front rooms.

Within twenty minutes, he'd walked through the entire lower floor of the Hopkins house. He'd spotted and committed to memory every entrance and exit.

There were four, counting the elevator.

Standing in Reginald Hopkins's office, he surveyed the banks of monitors and checked out the array of controls that took the place of a keyboard drawer in Hopkins's desk. Amelia's father had all the latest security measures. That was a good thing for Cole. It would be easier to keep up with people.

An unintelligible whisper tickled the edge of his brain. Cole glanced up, but just as he'd thought, he was alone.

He frowned as he mentally counted the controls before him. There was a touch-key for every monitor, every door in the house, even every TV. But there were a couple that didn't seem to do anything.

The whisper got a little louder. Cole closed his eyes and held his breath, listening, but he still couldn't tell what the disembodied voice was saying.

He touched a blank key, and a small virtual screen appeared with four blank spaces. It was a pass-code entry pad. Ninety percent of people used dangerously simple Personal Identification Numbers.

Cole had committed everything he could find out about Amelia and her father to memory—their birthdays, social security numbers, bank account numbers. So he started with the simplest. He keyed in Amelia's birth month and day, then pressed the key again.

A flutter of air cooled his cheek and he imagined he heard a faint tinkling laugh and smelled roses.

Try again.

Had he really heard those two words? He shook his head and entered the last four digits of her social security number. He heard an almost silent click, and the first three numbers on the keypad lit up.

Interesting. Was the system awaiting a second-level code? If so, the security was more sophisticated than he'd thought.

He spent some time studying the layout of the house and the location of the cameras. The distinct whir of the elevator reached his ears. He glanced at his watch. After seven. He drew his weapon and stalked over to the metal doors.

When the door slid open, he found himself staring into the snapping black eyes of a petite gray-haired lady. Behind her stood a young guard who looked as if he'd just been given detention by the school librarian.

"No reason whatsoever," the woman was saying. "Ought to have more respect for your elders."

Cole could have sworn he saw the young man's lips form the words, *Yes, ma'am.*

"And you—"

Cole's gaze snapped back to the tiny woman.

"Are you in charge? Because I intend to give you a piece of my mind. There's no reason to push people around." She stomped out of the elevator and looked around.

"What have you done with Amelia and Mr. Hopkins? You'd better not have hurt them or you'll answer to me."

Cole sighed in irritation. Another innocent life in his hands. And lucky him. She had a smart mouth and a keen eye, just like Amelia.

He caught the young guard's eye and nodded. "Go back to your post," he said.

The young man nodded in obvious relief. He turned on his heel and marched back into the elevator.

"Where is Amelia?" the woman demanded.

"Are you Mrs. Winston? The housekeeper?"

"Obviously you know that. Now are you going to answer my question?"

"Amelia's in her suite and Mr. Hopkins is in his."

Mrs. Winston propped her fists on her hips. "And what in blazes is going on here?"

Cole assessed her. If he were any kind of judge of people, he'd peg Mrs. Winston as fiercely patriotic and a closet romantic. He stepped closer to her, sent a covert glance around the room, then bent his head near her ear.

"Ma'am, this is a highly secret government undercover operation. We need your cooperation to save the U.S. from terrorists."

Mrs. Winston raised her right eyebrow and sent him a look that would wither an oak tree. "Right, and I'm the first lady. I'll thank you to not treat me like an idiot."

She paused for an instant, studying his face. "Is it really a government operation? Homeland Security?"

Cole suppressed a sigh of relief. He'd skirted dangerously close to the truth. It was a calculated risk—one he prayed would pay off in the long run. "I hope I can trust you? No one knows the truth except you."

Her head jerked up. "Not even—"

"Shh. Not even Amelia or Mr. Hopkins. I need someone I can depend on in case I have to get a message out. Can I depend on you?"

"I have to keep this secret from Amelia?"

Cole nodded solemnly. "It's for her own safety and the safety of the whole town."

"Oh." That revelation seemed to have stolen the

woman's tongue for an instant. "Why, I suppose so. Yes. I've never been one to tell tales out of school."

Cole let his relief show in his face this time. "Great. I can't tell you how worried I was that you wouldn't believe me."

The snapping black eyes narrowed. "Don't let anything happen to Amelia or Mr. Hopkins, or you'll have me to reckon with."

"Yes, ma'am."

Mrs. Winston surveyed the front room and her attention rested on a stain on the beautiful hardwood floor. "I suppose it's left to me to clean up all that blood, eh?"

Chapter Six

The main assembly room in the Hopkins Boatworks's office building buzzed with the murmurs of several dozen people—dock workers, assembly-line personnel, carpenters. They were Hopkins employees and Amelia knew them all.

She did not know the men standing at the doors with their arms crossed or their hands in their pockets, looking stern and threatening, like guards.

Like guards. *Ha.* They *were* guards. They were members of the Global Freedom Front. And she was about to deliver her employees into their traitorous, murdering hands.

To her right, her dad and the mayor stood flanked by two guards. To Amelia they both looked pale and terrified and the guards looked like armed terrorists. She turned her attention back to the crowd, trying to read their faces. What did they see? Was her face as pale as her father's?

"It's time," Cole whispered, laying a hand on her shoulder.

She was surprised she didn't cringe away from his

touch. But she'd rather be close to him than to the dark, mustached guard standing in a classic "at ease" position in front of the door behind them.

Like the other guards, he was dressed in a nondescript green uniform and lace-up black leather boots. They all looked like U.S. servicemen. Fear and guilt surged through her. What was she doing, standing in front of her employees, prepared to lie to them?

She stepped a little closer to Cole. For whatever reason—maybe because he'd saved her from Habib— his presence made her feel safe.

She knew the feeling was relative; Cole was safe only in comparison to Habib, or Chien Fou himself.

"Amelia?" Cole squeezed her shoulder. "The lives of these people are in your hands."

She cringed at that. But his words sank in.

She stepped forward to the front of the small dais. "Good morning," she called, raising her hand. "Good morning, everybody."

For an instant the murmurs got louder. Fabric rustled and chairs squeaked as the room's attention turned to her.

"Good morning," she repeated loudly, forcing a smile to her lips. "I have a very important announcement to make."

She had the whole room's attention. Looking out over the faces, she saw so many people she knew. Millie Simmons, whose husband had died in Iraq. Earl Boggan, an ex-con who'd come to her begging for a job, and who'd turned out to be a talented carpenter and a loyal employee.

Then her gaze lit on Joey Fancher, whose face was still streaked with tears from Amelia and Cole's early morning visit. It had broken Amelia's heart to have to tell him his big brother was dead.

What a bitter irony—that she had to betray him and the rest of her employees to save their lives.

Her throat closed up and she couldn't utter a word. A tiny, strangled moan escaped her lips.

Cole stepped closer. His breath fanned her cheek. "Trust me. You're doing the right thing."

"The right thing?" she whispered. "I'm signing their death warrants."

"Please, Amelia, trust me."

"Not as far as I can throw you," she snapped, then turned back to the crowd.

"Everybody. We've been given a huge—" She swallowed against the bile that threatened to rise in her throat. "A huge honor. But it's an honor that comes with sacrifice. Our government needs us. They're asking us to modify several HB-4200 motor yachts to act as…as decoys in case of a terrorist attack on major ports along the Eastern Seaboard."

The noise in the room rose as people nudged each other, whispered questions, turned to look at the guards.

"Okay, everybody. Please listen to me. This is a top-secret government mission, and we all must do our part. This is for…" Amelia paused again. Her heart felt as if it was bleeding, her mouth tasted like ashes. She took a deep breath. "This is for America."

She'd run out of strength and courage. Her eyes filled with tears and she turned to Cole.

He stepped forward. "Ladies and gentlemen, my name is Cole Robinson. I'm with Homeland Security."

Murmurs started up again, but Cole went on. "As

Amel—Ms. Hopkins said, this is a top-secret mission. A mission that depends on each one of you for its success. The mayor and Mr. Hopkins have sworn to do everything in their power to make this mission a success."

"Hey!" a voice from the back of the room called. "You sure you want the mayor on your side in this?"

A few people tittered. Amelia glanced at the mayor, who swayed slightly. The guard standing next to him took a small step closer to him.

Amelia quickly lay her hand on Cole's arm and stepped up to the dais again. "Mayor Wells is totally committed to the mission. Everyone knows that Camille, his beloved daughter and my best friend, is still in a coma. As much as he would rather be at her side, he's here, because what we're doing is of vital importance. And he knows, I know, and I hope you know—that Camille would be the first to tell her father to do everything in his power to protect America."

Cole nodded at her. "Anyone else got anything to say? Any questions?"

"What did you have to do with those damn pirates? I heard some people got hurt. And Ross Fancher is dead."

Loud mutterings broke out among the crowd, and a few others yelled, "Yeah," and "Good question."

"We weren't involved with the pirates, but we've dealt with them. And Fancher's death was tragic—an accident."

The mutterings faded. "Okay then," Cole continued. "Please, stand at attention. Each and every one of you is deputized as a Homeland Security agent. You cannot discuss any of this with family or friends. Not even with each other outside of this facility. You are taking an oath to protect the United States of America by not allowing one single word of this project to leave this room. Is that understood?"

"How're we supposed to keep this from our wives? Our families?"

Amelia spotted the speaker. It was Amos Biggs, a notorious grouch. He was a brilliant tool-and-die man, but he could see the downside of everything.

Still, Amelia wanted to know the answer to that question, too.

"You do it the same way our President does," Cole said without missing a beat. "The same way our special forces operatives do. The same way anyone who is working to keep our country free does it."

His uplifting, patriotic words almost sounded heart-felt. If only he believed them. Amelia pressed her lips together and held her breath, trying not to burst into tears.

If only he was the man he appeared to be at this moment. Tall, strong, with fervor in his voice and sincerity etched on his face. He could be the man she'd always dreamed of finding.

But he was a traitor, a liar, and for all she knew, a murderer.

"Is there anyone in this room who does not want to give their best to help protect America? If so, step up now, because we don't want anyone here who doesn't believe in freedom and the sacrifices we have to make to keep America free."

Of course, no one said a word.

Cole gave the bogus oath, and all the people in the room stood straight and tall as they repeated after him. Amelia's heart grew heavier and heavier.

When the oath was done, the whole room cheered, until Cole held up his hand. "One last thing, before we all go back to our jobs. The President is grateful to each and every one of you. He takes seriously the sacrifice you're making here—not being able to talk about what you're doing—not even with your family. When this is all over, each one of you will receive a personal letter, thanking you for your part in keeping America free."

The cheering grew louder, until it echoed in Amelia's ears like screams.

She turned toward her father, only to see him and the mayor being escorted out by guards.

"I have to get out of here," she muttered. She felt so helpless. The lives of her father, the mayor and every employee of Hopkins Boatworks, were in her hands. And she knew with absolute certainty that she wasn't up to the challenge. Sooner or later, her guilt and fear would get the best of her and she would let them down. The thought terrified her.

Cole pressed a warm, reassuring hand at the small of her back and led her out the door behind the dais.

"Where's your office?" he asked.

Amelia couldn't see anything but stars and darkness. A protective warmth enveloped her and before she knew what had happened, she was sitting in a chair in her office and someone was pressing a cup of cold water into her hand.

She opened her eyes and found herself looking down into Cole's storm-gray eyes. He was crouched in front of her chair, frowning at her.

"How'd we get here?"

"I think you fainted. Although you were able to walk—with a lot of help."

The protective warmth. It was Cole. She shuddered. "Don't ever touch me again." She sipped at the water and leaned back in the chair. A few stars still winked in and out before her eyes.

"No problem." His voice sounded muffled.

When Amelia opened her eyes, he'd moved away from her and propped a hip on the corner of her desk. His arms were crossed and he gazed down at her solemnly.

"What happened to you?" he asked. "Are you prone to fainting?"

Anger pricked her scalp and burned away the last of the stars. "No, I'm not."

She gulped the rest of the water down and tossed the paper cup toward a trash can. "I have never fainted in my life. I suppose being abducted by terrorists, attacked and finding out a friend of mine was murdered, not to mention being forced to present a heinous lie to my employees as truth sort of took its toll."

She lifted her chin and glared at him. "I can promise you it won't happen again."

Cole's eyes searched her face and then slid down her body all the way to her toes and back up. An odd look softened his harsh features for an instant before he clamped his jaw. "See that it doesn't."

He stood.

He filled up her little office. Even more than his broad shoulders and long lean body, his *presence* dominated the room. He was an imposing figure, in slacks and a dress shirt with the sleeves rolled back to reveal lean muscled forearms.

The perfect outfit for a meeting with blue-collar workers, she realized. He looked like a young executive, crisp and obviously in charge, but also accessible, with his open collar and rolled-up sleeves.

"Do they teach that in terrorist school?" she asked, inclining her head toward the front of his shirt.

He scowled. "Teach what?"

"How to dress to impress. You've got the look down. Even I could almost believe you were really a government agent on a mission from the President this morning."

His scowl grew deeper and darker. "This morning? I'm flattered. What about last night?"

She thought about his black pants and jacket and the wool fisherman's hat. "A seaman, definitely. So what's your terrorist uniform? Military gear and a belt of bullets?"

"Yeah. That's right." He stepped around her and reached for the doorknob. "Come on. I need to meet with Chien Fou and let him know how well you did." He turned and glared down at her. "In case you've got any bright ideas about being a hero, don't forget that if you make a mistake, or let something slip, your father will suffer."

"I have not forgotten that for one instant. Just like I've not forgotten who you really are under all that *Homeland Security* bull. I swear to you, Cole Robinson, when this is all over, you will pay. If I'm still alive, I'll be there at your execution."

Cole's eyes turned as black as coal. "It's a date."

THAT NIGHT Amelia was so tired she could barely keep her eyes open. Yet she couldn't sleep.

She was worried about her father. He was acting strange—too quiet, too obsequious. She was afraid one of the guards had hurt him. But when she asked, he'd sworn to her they'd been polite. They'd even removed his and the mayor's handcuffs as soon as they'd gone to his suite. When she'd turned to Cole with a questioning look, he'd nodded reassuringly. She prayed he was telling her the truth.

Finally, after a strained dinner with the mayor and her father where no one said a word, Amelia stood and tried to excuse herself, claiming exhaustion.

"Sorry, Amelia. We're meeting with Chien Fou in his suite."

Amelia's heart sank. She'd hoped to take a long shower to wash the taint of lies off her, then check on her father to make sure he took his evening medications.

Cole waited for her to precede him up the stairs. Behind her, she heard the guards ordering the mayor and her father to follow them.

"What is this, some kind of command performance? Why didn't he come to dinner?" Like it mattered to her. But she did want to understand as much about Chien Fou as she could. She knew that the number one credo of war was *know your enemy*.

And this was war.

"He eats alone. His bodyguard oversees the preparation."

She turned on the first stair. "I'll bet that thrilled Mrs. Winston."

Cole's lips twitched. "Yeah. That lady's not afraid to speak her mind, is she?"

Amelia looked away. Thinking about what his eyes

would do if he smiled, would get her nowhere. Instead, she thought about Chien Fou's eating habits.

"So what's Chien Fou's problem?" she asked. "Is he allergic to something?"

"I've never been able to find out. He could be paranoid about being poisoned. He's like that. You'll notice he never goes anywhere without two bodyguards."

"I guess it's a dangerous life being an international terrorist."

"Keep your voice down. You need to watch what you say. Chien Fou has no sense of humor and a hair-trigger temper."

At the top of the stairs, a stony-faced guard led them to the upstairs master suite. He rapped once on the double doors.

Another guard opened the doors and stood back so they could enter. Chien Fou sat in the sitting room, his meal tray at his elbow. As they entered, he nodded to the guard who stood next to his chair. The man picked up the tray and took it out of the suite.

"Ah, Miss Hopkins. I understand you handled yourself very well this morning. You even fielded a disparaging comment about your mayor."

Amelia didn't respond. She might be this traitor's enemy, but she didn't have to engage in conversation with him.

Behind her, her father and the mayor were led in. She stepped sideways and linked her arm through her dad's and squeezed. A ghost of a smile touched his pale face and he squeezed back.

"Ah. Good evening, Mayor Wells, Mr. Hopkins. How kind of you to join us."

Amelia noticed that Cole was standing with his hands clasped behind him in the at ease military posture. But somehow she knew that he was anything but at ease. She could feel his tension across the couple of feet that separated them. She wondered if Chien Fou could feel it.

"Miss Hopkins, you might not have been so quick to defend your mayor if you knew about our relationship."

Her gaze snapped back to Chien Fou. "Your relationship?"

"Excellent. I have your attention now."

Out of the corner of her eye, she saw the mayor run a finger inside the collar of his shirt.

"Yes, it's quite fascinating. I'm sure you haven't forgotten the recent tragedy in Raven's Cliff."

"I had no idea that Fisher's research was tainting the fish," Mayor Wells blurted. A guard immediately appeared at his side.

Chien Fou glanced at the mayor, then turned his black eyes back to Amelia. "As I was saying, the incident with the fish brought the mayor and I together—"

"I never saw you before—"

The guard backhanded Mayor Wells across the mouth, spraying blood.

Amelia gasped and pulled her father closer.

Chien Fou gave the guard a tiny shake of his head. "Mayor Wells," he said, "I don't believe anyone was talking to you."

The mayor wiped a hand across his lip and looked at the blood.

"Were they?"

Amelia heard the threat underneath the monotone voice of the terrorist. The mayor was only seconds away from death. She prayed he had sense enough to realize that. She didn't want her best friend Camille to wake up from her coma to find her father dead.

"Miss Hopkins. I see you're having a hard time believing that Mayor Wells so completely betrayed his constituency. Well, believe it."

Amelia lifted her chin.

Chien Fou laughed. "You are a brave young woman. I hope your bravery doesn't overshadow your common sense. It can get you killed if you're not careful." He waved a hand and one of the guards poured him a glass of water.

"Now, to business. Mr. Hopkins, I need a blueprint of the modifications that will be needed to adapt your boats to transport the explosive without incident. We will need seven boats."

Before her father could respond, Amelia broke in. "My father and I will work on the plan together. We can have a blueprint developed by—"

"By this time tomorrow," Chien Fou interrupted.

"That's not possible," her father said. Amelia squeezed his arm, but he shook off her warning.

"I beg your pardon?" Chien Fou's voice held that deadly undercurrent again.

"It's impossible to make that kind of modification within days, much less hours. And anyway, what makes you think I would voluntarily help your terrorist plot?"

Chien Fou sneered and sat forward. "Your daughter's safety, for one thing."

"Why you—"

The guard standing behind them stepped up and put a gun to Reginald Hopkins's neck.

"Dad!" Amelia cried. She turned to Chien Fou. "Stop it. We'll manage. We'll figure something out. Just don't hurt my father. Please."

"Amelia, don't beg him for anything. I don't care what they do to me." He directed his attention to Chien Fou. "I'll do what you ask. But you have to give me your word that my daughter will be safe."

Chien Fou smiled. "Of course. I have no problem giving you my word." He took a sip of water. "Now please, take them away. I'm tired."

The guard pocketed his weapon. "Let's go," he said.

Amelia took her dad's hand and turned toward the door. As they were herded out of the room, she heard Chien Fou say, "Cole, stay a moment. We haven't had a game of chess in a while."

Cole nodded at Chien Fou but his attention was on Amelia's back. It was straight and dignified and achingly vulnerable.

"Cole."

He gave Chien Fou his full attention. Damn, he hated the man. Sometimes he wished this were a CIA operation rather than a Homeland Security one. He didn't understand why the government didn't order him eliminated.

Okay, he did understand. The target wasn't just Chien Fou. It was the entire organization. The Global Freedom Front had survived the deaths of two leaders, and if they couldn't seriously cripple the organization, it would survive Chien Fou's death, too.

"What's the story with Miss Hopkins?" Chien Fou asked.

"The story?" *Ah, hell. Pay attention,* he admonished himself. Chien Fou wasn't going to like that snappy response.

Sure enough, the GFF leader's mouth curled into a sneer. "Watch yourself, Cole. I find you extremely capable, but you are not indispensable."

"No, Leader."

"Well?"

"Miss Hopkins is intelligent, highly intuitive and resourceful. She's the one who will be able to keep the employees in line."

"Excellent." Chien Fou waved, and the guard standing at his left hand poured him another glass of water. He used a different glass. "Secure her cooperation."

"We have it, Leader." Cole didn't like the tone in Chien Fou's voice. He was a strange, diabolical man. Cole had never been able to pinpoint just what was askew in the terrorist's brain. But he knew he never wanted to know everything about the man who called himself Mad Dog.

Chien Fou's black eyes glittered. "Please listen to me, Cole. *Secure* it. By whatever means necessary. Use seduction or force, or fear, I don't care. But neutralize her power. If she's all that you seem to believe she is, she's already plotting a way to stop us."

As soon as Amelia turned the dead bolt on her suite doors, something broke loose inside her.

Her chest squeezed, her throat clogged, her eyes burned. For a moment, she sat on the edge of the bed with her hands over her mouth while the horror of the past twenty-four hours flew across her vision in fast-forward mode. Up to and including the shocking sight she'd just witnessed of a gun barrel pressed to her father's neck.

She rubbed her eyes as tears began to well.

No. No crying. She stood and paced, breathing deeply, doing her best to control herself, but it was no use. The tears kept coming.

Everything—the attack, Ross's death and now the imminent threat to her father, came down on her head at once, and she lost it.

Sobbing, she made her way into the bathroom. She stripped and stepped into the shower, letting the jets of hot water wash her tears down the drain. Not even the penetrating steam could wash away her fear, though.

She was such a coward. Here she was, soaking her tense muscles and exhausted brain in a luxurious shower when Ross was dead and the town of Raven's Cliff was once again in the clutches of evil. She lifted her face to the hot spray.

A horrible thought occurred to her. What if the legend was true? What if there really was a curse on Raven's Cliff—an eternal curse? And Cole was caught up in the evil, like everyone else?

Trust him, trust him, trust him. The jets beat a staccato rhythm against the glass brick walls of the shower—a sound she'd never noticed before. And a faint scent of roses tickled her nostrils.

Trust him? She turned off the shower. Trust Cole? Why would that possibility even enter her head?

He'd asked her to trust him just as she was about to speak to her employees. Now, her exhausted brain was searching for a way to protect her father. That was all.

Dear heavens, how she wished she could make his tale of a Homeland Security mission to protect the Eastern Seaboard real. Was it possible? He'd seemed so sincere, so passionate about America and freedom when he was talking to her employees.

As Amelia stepped out of the shower, she swayed. She had to steady herself with a hand on the vanity. Too much hot water. She shouldn't have stayed in there so long.

She wrapped an oversize bath towel around her and sat on her vanity bench. For a few seconds she rested her head on her knees, until the shadows at the edge of her vision disappeared.

Trust him. She lifted her head. She could almost believe she'd heard a whisper, and the rosy scent still tickled her nostrils. She didn't remember buying anything that smelled like that. Where had she noticed that scent before?

COLE FELT NAUSEOUS as he headed downstairs to Amelia's suite. He understood perfectly what the Leader had been talking about. He wanted Cole to break her.

Cole had witnessed Chien Fou's orders being carried out before.

But this time he was the one tasked with the job, and if he didn't do it, Chien Fou would send someone else— someone who wouldn't balk at harming a woman.

Abel was standing guard outside Amelia's doors.

"What are you doing here?" Cole demanded.

"Orders. Leader wants to be certain nobody goes wandering around the house alone."

"Fine," he said. "I'm here now."

Abel nodded.

Cole unlocked the doors and slipped inside. The room's darkness was relieved only by the sliver of light shining around the edge of the bathroom door.

A picture rose up before his inner vision. Amelia, standing in the shower, the spray like diamonds on her creamy skin, her breasts high and tight, her belly slightly rounded. Water running in rivulets down, down, between her breasts, down her abdomen and farther, until it trickled between her legs—

Damn it! Damn Chien Fou's sadistic, perverse mind. Chien Fou's suggestion had disgusted Cole. He'd never in his life used force or fear against a woman, and he never would.

But for some reason one word Chien Fou had used had stuck in his mind. *Seduction.*

He turned on the overhead lights, hoping their brightness would burn away the thoughts of Amelia's slender, perfect body. He wasn't here to satisfy his horny urges. He wasn't even here to protect Amelia—although he would.

He was here to stop the Global Freedom Front. And he knew in the war against terror, there were always sacrifices.

AMELIA JUMPED as a brisk rapping sounded at the bathroom door.

"Amelia?"

It was Cole.

"Don't come in."

"Are you all right?"

She wiped her face with a corner of the towel. "Of

course," she said as strongly as she could. "I just needed a shower."

She hadn't expected him back so soon.

She quickly dried off and wrapped her terry-cloth robe around her. She ran a comb through her wet hair and squeezed water from the ends. Then she took a deep breath and opened the door.

If possible, Cole looked more exhausted than she felt. He sat on the edge of the bed, his elbows propped on his knees, his head in his hands.

"Are you all right?"

For a moment he didn't move. Finally he pushed his fingers through his hair and stood. "Yeah. Just tired."

"Yes, well. It must be exhausting to betray your country."

Cole stood and glowered at her. "Your sarcasm is getting to be annoying."

"Sorry. But it's the only weapon left in my arsenal."

"Amelia…"

She swallowed hard against the lump that had formed in her throat. She was still close to tears, but she'd be damned if she'd cry in front of him.

He walked across the room and looked out the windows. "What did your dad say?"

She pressed her lips together for an instant and blinked away the stinging in her eyes. "About what?"

"The blueprints. Modifying the boats."

"He didn't say anything. He—" She stopped.

Cole turned. "What's the matter?"

He was silhouetted by the faint glow of moonlight that shone in the window. He looked powerful, like a warrior. And he exuded confidence and trust.

She wanted desperately to tell him about her father, about how worried she was that Chien Fou would harm him. But he was the enemy. She kept forgetting that.

"Amelia?"

"You kept Dad's heart attack secret from Chien Fou. Why?"

He didn't answer right away. "It seemed important to you to hide it, and it made no difference to him."

Trust him.

"He's been so depressed since his heart attack. You already figured out that he couldn't finish the new design."

Cole crossed his arms. "So what are you saying?"

"Will you promise me you'll do everything in your power to protect him?"

A harsh laugh was her answer. She pressed her fingertips against her mouth.

"Why would you even ask me that? I'm a terrorist, or have you forgotten?"

"There's no one else to ask." Her voice was muffled by her hand.

"Not a very good reason to trust someone—because there's no one else."

"I know." She wouldn't tell him the other reason she was compelled to trust him. She would never tell anyone about the voice of the fortune-teller in her ear and the smell of spicy, rosy incense that wafted around her each time she heard the woman's voice.

He stood silent for a few moments. Even though the room was dark, she knew he was studying her.

"How much do you know about the boats?"

"A lot. I've watched him design boats my whole life. And he never got impatient with me. He answered all my questions, let me sit on his lap while he worked." She took a shaky breath. "I couldn't design one from scratch, but I know the models inside and out."

"You and I can work out how to store and hide the explosive."

Relief washed over her like the tide coming in. "I don't understand why you're doing this, but I have no other choice but to trust you. Please protect my father as long as you can."

"As long as I can?"

She nodded as the tears she'd been holding back ever since he'd come into the room began to spill from her eyes. "I know we're not going to get out of this alive. But don't let them hurt him. Please."

"Amelia…"

The slow, sexy way he drew out her name sent longing humming deep within her. She wiped the tears off her cheeks and waited for what he was going to say. But all he did was look down at his feet, shove his hands into his pockets like a kid who'd just knocked a baseball through a window and hunch his shoulders.

After a long pause, he lifted his head enough to catch her gaze. "Just hold on, Amelia. Okay? Just hold on. It'll all be over soon."

His words struck fear in her heart. She opened her mouth to fire a retort back at him, but she couldn't. She couldn't say a word.

"I'm taking a shower." He picked up a small duffel bag she hadn't noticed before and headed into the bathroom.

Amelia sat down on the edge of the bed and closed

her eyes, waiting for the voice inside her head to re-assure her one more time—to tell her she could trust him. But the voice didn't come.

Chapter Seven

Cole turned the bathroom light out before he opened the door. He'd stayed in the shower for what seemed like an hour. He'd been up for thirty-six hours and he was so tired his bones ached. Like Amelia, he'd hardly been able to lift a fork to his mouth at dinner, although he had to admit that Mrs. Winston made boiled beef taste like manna from heaven.

When he'd finally exited the steamy shower stall, he'd looked at his two days' growth of beard in the mirror, debating whether to shave it or leave it. It was dark, like his hair, and gave him a sinister look that fit in with the other GFF members.

But he hated whiskers, especially short prickly ones. They itched. So he'd shaved. After all, he was playing the part of a clean-cut patriotic guy—a Homeland Security agent.

Patriotic guy? Sure, he was a patriotic guy, for all the good that did him. As he slipped through the bathroom door into Amelia's bedroom, he regretted shaving. Even a couple days' growth of beard hid his face a little.

And hiding was what he did best these days. He'd pushed his boss for an undercover assignment after the highly publicized trial of his father—for treason. Senator Robinson had been selling information to a fringe group for years. Never much, just enough to pad his income so he could live—and party—like a rock star.

Thanks, Dad.

Cole stood with his back against the bathroom door until his eyes adjusted to the dark. The faint light of the moon shone in Amelia's windows, lending a pale dusting of silver to everything in the room, including her hair.

She lay with her back to him, the satin sheets draping her sweetly curved hips that rose enticingly from her small waist. Her hair spilled over the pillow and glimmered in the moonlight.

His body reacted to the sight of her lying in bed. He groaned silently and clamped his jaw.

Not going there. Not now. Not ever.

Where was he going to sleep? Not that it mattered. He could sleep in a nest of vipers tonight.

It looked as if his choices were a dainty chaise longue, a tiny antique desk chair or the floor. He didn't dare try the first two. So the floor it was. Despite what he'd just told himself about the nest of vipers, he sent a longing look at the vast unused expanse of king-size bed before he stepped over to the entry alcove. He might as well sleep near the door, in case something happened.

"Cole?"

Her sleepy voice startled him.

"Sorry," he said. "I didn't mean to wake you."

"You didn't. I mean, I was drifting in and out."

"I'm settling down. I won't bother you again. Go back to sleep."

She didn't say anything. He grabbed a throw pillow from the chaise and tossed it onto the floor.

"Cole?"

The soft drowsy word sent a sharp thrill through his groin and put him right in the middle of where he'd promised himself he wouldn't go.

Her voice held just the right tone of languid seductiveness, although he knew for a fact she didn't intend it to sound that way. Just as she didn't intend to look like a teasing seductress, lying in the moonlight with her back to him.

Snap out of it, he commanded himself. *You already scare her half to death just by being here. If she thought for a second that you were sexually attracted to her, she'd—*

"Do you want to sleep here?"

Her words nearly knocked him for a loop. His jaw dropped open. "Wh-what?"

She turned over and sat up, pulling the satin sheets up to her chin. "Look." She waved her hand. "I don't use a third of this super-king-size bed."

He saw her eyes glitter in the pale light. "If you were going to— I mean, I figure you'd have already done it. So I'm trusting you to…you know, be a gentleman."

Son of a— How she'd decided she could trust him, he didn't know. He *knew* he couldn't trust himself.

"Okay. Thanks." *Okay? Thanks,* for God's sake?

What the hell was wrong with him? If he had a lick of sense, he'd sleep on the other damn side of the door to her suite. But the thought of a real, comfortable bed overcame his good sense.

He looked down at his white T-shirt and gray sweatpants, and decided he was decent enough to lie on the edge of the bed farthest from her, especially if he stayed on top of the covers.

Well, decent if you didn't count the bulge in his pants. He glared at it and held his breath until it began to wane. Then he lay down gingerly on the very edge of the bed. A quiet groan escaped his lips. Every inch of his body hurt. And damn it all to hell, her bed was comfortable.

"Are you all right?"

Don't turn over this way.

She didn't, but that didn't stop her voice from floating along his nerve endings like a spark of lightning, enticing him.

"Yeah. Just bone-tired, and this bed feels like heaven."

"I know. I can't believe how frail humans are. We can't function very long without sleep."

Cole knew from experience just about exactly how long a body could function without sleep. He'd done it once, when he'd had to run from a lunatic who'd thought he was part of an international terrorist cell, and who, luckily for Cole, ran himself to death before Cole's body gave out.

"Yeah. Sometimes it seems as if you can substitute one thing for another—if you can't sleep you can eat, or vice versa."

What do you substitute for sex? His body wanted to know.

"I suppose so…" Amelia's voice trailed off.

Cole lifted his head, but her back was to him and he couldn't tell if she'd fallen asleep. He sighed and relaxed a little further into the bed.

"What's going to happen tomorrow?"

He jumped. Had he already begun to drift off? Without moving, he spoke. "We've got to work out a plan for modifying the boats to hold the explosive. But we can worry about that tomorrow. Tonight we need to sleep."

"You really did a great job of lying to my employees," she commented.

"Is this where I say thank you?"

She turned and sat back against the headboard. "How do you expect a hundred people to keep such a huge secret? What kind of plan is it that depends on the hostages hiding their own imprisonment?"

He didn't answer.

She crossed her legs into a half-lotus position. "Oh, dear heavens, that's what you're counting on, isn't it? You know they're going to go home and tell their spouses. By tomorrow the whole town will be in on the big, secret government plot to save the country from terrorists. And that will ensure that they'll keep it to themselves. Oh—" She covered her mouth with her hands. She shook her head. "I can't do this. I can't be a part of it. You're using these people's patriotism to force them to betray their country. And all the time letting them believe they're working for freedom."

Horror and contempt dripped from her muffled words. Amelia hated him for what she thought he was doing. And rightly so.

He gave up on his quixotic effort to keep his eyes

closed and looked at her. The sheet covered her lower body, but he could see the little cotton tank top she wore. Her skin glowed in the moonlight. She looked like an angel. A very sexy angel. The shadows were deep but he could still see the hollow between her breasts and the outline of her nipples under the thin cotton.

His body stirred again. He closed his eyes but her afterimage was burned onto his retinae.

"What if it were true?" he muttered. He clenched his jaw—too late. Oh, hell. He lay totally still, hoping against hope that she hadn't heard his quiet words.

For a long moment everything was quiet. He couldn't even hear her breathing over the rapid beating of his heart. A relieved sigh escaped his lips. She was asleep. She hadn't heard him.

"What did you say?" Her voice was hesitant, hopeful, distrustful.

"Nothing," he growled, turning his back to her. "Go to sleep. We've got to make floating bombs tomorrow."

"DO THEY HAVE TO GO with us everywhere?" Amelia whispered to Cole as she walked through the small office complex and out into the clean room, where seven luxurious HB-4200 motor yachts were waiting for interior finish work. Three Global Freedom Front guards followed them.

"They look as if they have guns under those military jackets. It's going to scare my employees and make them suspicious."

"The guards do have guns, Amelia. Don't forget for one minute who these people are. They're deliberately dressed to resemble U.S. military special forces—at least the Hollywood version. And people are familiar with it. Look at your employees' faces. This military presence is impressing the hell out of them."

Amelia's gut clenched. "That's great. And how many of them are going to die because they believe I would never betray them?"

Cole caught her arm and turned her toward him. He glanced around and then bent his head to look her straight in the eye. "I'm doing my best to see that nobody else dies. But, Amelia, you're the key. You *have* to make each and every person who works for you believe that what we're doing is for America's safety. And to make them believe it, you've got to believe it. A little bit anyhow."

"I wish I could. I wish I could banish the reality of Ross's death. Banish the sound of that gunshot in my living room that killed Habib. I wish these…feelings I have—" Amelia paused, appalled by what she'd let slip out.

Cole stared at her. "Feelings?"

It took a superhuman effort not to cut and run. But every eye in the clean room was on her. She had a part to play, and her employees' lives depended on her giving an Oscar-worthy performance.

"I meant, feelings—well, more like wishes that the lies you're telling me—us are true." She was completely out of breath by the time she finished.

"Believe it, Amelia. Believe it inside. That's the best way to protect your employees. They'll follow your lead."

"That's what I'm afraid of. Am I leading them to their deaths?"

"Amelia?"

She turned. "Uncle Marvin? What are you doing here? Why aren't you out fishing?" She kissed his cheek.

"Hard to fish when the town's in such an uproar. Everybody's talking so loud it's scaring the fish."

Amelia's pulse sped up. "Really?"

The septuagenarian's brows lowered. "Don't be flip with me, Amelia. You know that everybody came home from the boatyard yesterday with a top-secret story about terrorist plots and Homeland Security and—"

"Marvin? Sorry I don't know your last name. I'm Cole Robinson." Cole held out his hand.

"Cole, this is Marvin Smith, my ersatz uncle. He raised my father after my grandparents died at sea."

Marvin gave Cole the level of scrutiny he'd give a two-headed fish.

To his credit, Cole didn't flinch, but Amelia could feel his discomfort. She'd never been the object of Marvin Smith's mistrust, but she'd seen its effects. It spoke to Cole's self-confidence and assurance that he didn't break.

The two stared at each other for several seconds. Then Marvin spoke. "I heard you had nothing to do with the pirates that tore up the town the other night."

Cole straightened. "That's right, sir. I'm with Homeland Security. We actually stopped the pirates. We're planning a counter-terrorist attack based on information we've gathered from undercover operatives. We need several of Hopkins's yachts to carry out this important mission."

"So you took over the town." Marvin's keen eyes checked out the three guards who were standing at attention just within earshot.

"It's a vital mission, sir."

Again, Amelia felt herself being sucked into Cole's lies. He was so sincere, so impassioned, when he started in on his Homeland Security cover, unlike the stiff, somber terrorist.

"Hard to believe the U.S. government would pick a place like Raven's Cliff for such an important mission."

"The very fact that Raven's Cliff is small and isolated makes it perfect. We can modify the boats here without anyone knowing what we're doing, and then we'll have harmless-looking pleasure boats that will be able to stop a terrorist plot we know is brewing."

Amelia stared at Cole in amazement. He could definitely spin a tale. He'd just taken the basics of everything the Global Freedom Front was planning to do, and turned it into a patriotic mission to save America.

Marvin wasn't so impressed. His grizzled brows were still lowered and his sharp gaze was narrowed. "I'm not so sure it's a good thing for the town. This has been a long, tragic summer."

Cole sent her a questioning glance, then centered all his attention on Marvin. "Tragic?"

Marvin nodded. "You mean, Amelia didn't tell you? Raven's Cliff has lived under a curse for years. For generations, the old lighthouse has been haunted by the ghost of a sea captain who lost his family at sea. Then five years ago the lighthouse keeper was killed in a fire. Earlier this summer we had a serial killer who killed several lovely young women in town. And there's more that I won't even get into." Marvin rubbed his hands together. "Kind of odd that you people would show up here right now."

"Sir, let me assure you that my job is to keep Raven's Cliff safe, and I pledge to do everything in my power to ensure the safety of the residents."

"Then what happened to young Ross Fancher?" Marvin probed. "How did he end up dead?"

Cole shook his head solemnly. "It was a freak accident. He fell and hit his head on a cleat."

"Freak accident, huh? Ross's been around boats his whole life. Hard to believe he'd come to his end on a boat."

Cole just nodded.

"Amelia, where's Reg? I'm starting to get worried about him."

"He's—"

Cole broke in. "He's up in the cliff house, which our commander is using as a base of operations. He and the mayor are helping with the planning and execution of the project."

"So that's what happened to the mayor. Your commander might want to watch his back. Raven's Cliff's illustrious leader is not so illustrious."

"Sir?"

"Mayor Wells got himself involved in some shady deals. Sad story. Amelia can tell you. The mayor's daughter is her best friend. That poor girl was missing for months. She's been found now, but she's in a coma."

Cole shook his head. "Raven's Cliff has certainly had its troubles."

"Aye," Marvin replied. "And I'm afraid they're not over yet. Which is why I don't get what's going on here. Why would the government involve innocent citizens in this level of antiterrorist activity? Sounds too dangerous, and too iffy. I'm not sure I like this idea."

Amelia waited to hear what Cole's answer to that was. Uncle Marvin was far more savvy than his simple fisherman facade would indicate.

"Sir, I can assure you that Homeland Security is on top of this. We don't intend to put innocent lives in danger."

"Son, in times of war, innocent lives are always in danger."

Cole forced himself to look the elderly fisherman in the eye. Marvin Smith held his gaze for a few seconds, then nodded.

After he left to go up to the cliff house, Cole suppressed a sigh of relief. He'd passed some kind of test. He wasn't sure what Marvin had been looking for, but good or bad, he'd gotten his answer.

Cole wished he knew what the question was.

Damn, he'd spun a web of lies. He was sick of lying. Sick of kowtowing to Chien Fou. But more than anything, he was sick of seeing hatred and contempt in Amelia's eyes.

He cleared his throat. "Marvin seems like a great guy," he said.

"He's more than a great guy." Her voice was icy.

Cole looked down the row of yachts. The enormity of what they were doing almost overwhelmed him. They were going to turn these innocent-looking pleasure boats into fifty-foot floating bombs. Homeland Security's plan was to stop them before the GFF could detonate the explosive, but from the instant the detonator was put into place, each one of these fifty-foot yachts was an incendiary device that could blow a hole in a supertanker.

He thought about his meeting with Reginald Hopkins this morning, and how hesitant and distracted the man had been. "After talking with your dad this morning, I see what you mean about him." Cole kept his voice low and his stance casual. He didn't want the guard to hear their conversation, but he didn't want them to think he was acting suspicious, either.

Amelia crossed her arms. "He's depressed. He's ill. He can't focus on anything. Hasn't been able to since his heart attack fifteen months ago. Do you see why I didn't want anyone to know about his illness? If that monster up there—" she gestured toward the cliff house "—figures out that Dad can't help him, what's he going to do? Have him shot?"

"Lower your voice," Cole snapped, resisting the urge to glance toward the guards.

Her eyes widened and she clamped her mouth shut.

"It's okay. You were whispering…sort of."

"Do you think they heard me?"

Cole shook his head. He wanted to touch her, to reassure her. Wipe the fear from her eyes. But that was impossible, and not only because they were under scrutiny.

Because he had put that fear there.

"Can we get into one of the boats?" he asked, working to force his attention back to his mission. "Look at possibilities for hiding the explosive?"

She nodded. "The two on the end aren't finished inside yet." She sent him a cold glance before turning and walking down the row of boats.

He followed, acutely aware of the guards' eyes on them. He prayed they wouldn't follow them. He needed to inspect the boat's interior without arousing suspicion.

Amelia stopped at the sixth boat. She waved at a man

who was working at a large table, measuring and cutting upholstery material. "Hi, Isaac. How's Jeanie doing?"

He looked up with a smile, which faded when he saw Cole and the guards.

"She's fine, Miss Hopkins. She wanted to thank you for the baby stuff you sent over."

Amelia laughed.

The sound pierced Cole's heart like an arrow. He almost clutched at his chest. He'd never heard anything like Amelia's laugh before. And he wanted to hear it again.

"You're both very welcome for the 'baby stuff.' Be sure and let us know when you need to take time off. Your supervisor already knows to expect it."

"Thanks." Isaac went back to cutting.

Amelia grabbed the handrail of a ladder and started climbing.

More shocks to his system. His mouth went dry at the perfect view of her curvy bottom moving as she climbed. Her jeans did wonderful things for her hips and legs. She reached the top and pulled herself over into the boat, then turned and looked down at him.

"Aren't you coming?"

He shook off the image her unintended double entendre put in his head, and quickly climbed up and over. A casual glance told him the guards had moved into position at the base of the ladder, but for the moment at least, they were staying put.

"This is the deck," she said crisply, as if she were giving a tour. Her back was stiff. She exuded disapproval, even condemnation.

And he understood why. She was being forced to participate in a plot to ruin the American economy.

"I don't think we can hide the explosives up here anywhere. What's underneath me?"

"I'll show you." She headed down into the salon, so he followed, and saw immediately why Hopkins Yachts were in demand worldwide. There was a bright, spacious main salon. Even without the upholstery, it was obvious that this was a superbly built, quality product.

"There's the main salon here, with the galley. Two sleeping cabins, one fore and one aft. We have ample stowage along the sides, and of course, the bilge below. Do you know how you plan to—" Amelia's voice cracked. Her arms were tightly folded. Her back ramrod-stiff. She was close to her breaking point.

But Cole had to push forward. He needed the information about the boats, because he had to report back to Chien Fou that evening.

"We're using C-4. You probably know about it from movies. We have it packaged in hundred-pound blocks. C-4 is malleable, so it can be packed into tight places and molded if necessary for maximum directional destruction." He examined the settee frames that were awaiting upholstery. Behind each seat was a hefty amount of empty storage space. He measured it with his eyes. "This area here could easily hold three hundred pounds of C-4. We figure that should be enough to blow a small hole in a supertanker."

"A *small* hole?"

He nodded. "An oil supertanker has a double steel hull. Purposely built so they're very difficult to penetrate."

"I know that," she said stiffly.

"Then you know that it doesn't take a large hole to

create a massive oil spill. It just takes a concentrated blast to be sure both outer and inner hulls are compromised." He glanced around the salon. "We can pack the C-4 on the right side of each boat."

"Starboard side," Amelia said.

He raised his brows.

"Not right or left. Starboard and port. No matter which direction you're facing, the designation stays the same. Apparently you're not much of a sailor."

"I'm no engineer, either, but I figure we have to counterweight the *starboard* side with something."

"Lead. We have hundred-pound lead blocks that we use to adjust the boat's waterline. If we insert them into the port side, they'll counter the weight of the C-4. That way the boats will float true on the waterline and be easier to steer."

Amelia's voice was choked. He assessed her. She was standing too straight, too stiff. Her knees were locked.

"Okay, so who handles this? I need to talk to him and put him in touch with Klauss, our munitions expert."

She didn't answer him. Her hand went to her temple.

Cole rose from his crouch just in time to catch her. He swept her up into his arms and maneuvered through the small door into the forward berth and lowered her gently onto the king-size bed.

Her hair tumbled in tangles over her face. He brushed them aside. Her skin was cool. He had no idea if that was a good thing or not. Cradling her cheek in his palm, he leaned close.

"Amelia?" he whispered.

Her honey-brown eyes opened. For a second they were unfocused. Then she met his gaze.

"Wha— What are you doing?"

"You fainted."

"I did not faint," she said shakily, struggling to sit up.

Cole backed away and sat on a settee beside the bed. "You fainted, and if I hadn't caught you, you'd have hit your head on the table. And it's no wonder. You haven't eaten a bite in the two days I've been here. You were already worried sick about your dad. And now all this."

"*All this?* You mean, all this that *you've* brought down on our heads? All this C-4 explosive you're going to pack into my boats and send off to wreck the American economy? And for what? What's your beef against America, Cole Robinson? You were born here, weren't you?"

Cole wiped a hand down his face. He ought to just stay quiet and get her out of here. Despite the autumn crispness in the air, here on the yacht inside the metal warehouse, the temperature was probably in the nineties. Another contributing factor to her fainting spell.

But she was staring at him with those honey-brown eyes and he felt the urge to act heroic, even if he wasn't.

"Amelia, I wish there was a way to convince you to trust me. Give you some assurance that there's a way out of this nightmare—for you and your father. For your employees."

Her eyes turned as cold as brown bottle glass. "But there's not, is there?"

He had no answer for her.

"Is there?"

The soft hesitation in her voice gave him renewed

hope. He could *not* tell her the truth. He'd taken an oath. But he could come close. He could give her hints. He could *make* her trust him.

Couldn't he?

"Don't give up on me, okay? Not yet."

"Cole?"

There were a million questions in that one syllable. A hundred-thousand pleas. And he couldn't answer even one of them.

"Amelia, please believe me, I don't want to lie to you. If I could tell you who I really am, I would."

She looked at his mouth.

Damn it, she wasn't—

Oh, hell yeah, she was.

Before he could make a conscious decision to back away, she leaned forward, close enough that he could feel her mouth trembling. He was caught. Stuck there by the temptation of those luscious lips. That tiny beauty mark at one corner that he hadn't noticed until just now.

He moved a millimeter and his mouth touched hers. He gasped.

So did she.

A heavy thud crashed into his brain. Jerking back, he tried to make sense of the sound while at the same time moving to shield Amelia.

"What's going on here?"

Alarm fired along his nerve endings. *Abel.* One of Chien Fou's trusted guards. He was standing right in the door to the stateroom. How had he boarded the boat without Cole hearing him? And how long had he been standing there?

Had Abel heard his last words to Amelia? If he had, he may have just sealed both their fates.

"We were looking at storage spaces in the boat and Miss Hopkins grew faint."

"Yeah?" Abel scowled at them. "Well, it's time to get back to the house. You've got a meeting with Chien Fou this evening, and you'd better be ready."

Cole prayed Abel was referring to the information about how to plant the explosive on the yachts, and not an explanation of why he was saying things to Amelia that a terrorist working for the Global Freedom Front would never say.

As he guided Amelia out of the stateroom and up the galley ladder, Abel's mutter reached his ears.

"You'd better watch yourself, Robinson. You're treading on thin ice already. You think Chien Fou doesn't know who you are?"

Chapter Eight

When Cole and Amelia arrived in Chien Fou's suite, he was in his usual position in the sitting room of the upstairs master suite, flanked by his personal guards. His black eyes glittered above that sinister smile.

Amelia was still shaky from her fainting spell earlier, even though Cole had marched her straight into the kitchen as soon as they got to the house.

Mrs. Winston had made her eat a plate of pasta with Parmesan cream sauce and drink a glass of sweet tea. The food made her feel better at the time, but now it sat heavily in her stomach. It didn't help that Chien Fou's suite was stifling hot. She took a deep breath but it didn't help, it was like breathing in a sauna.

"Miss Hopkins, tell me how you plan to secrete the C-4 in the boats."

Chien Fou's oily voice sent fear skittering down her spine. Before she could force enough breath to speak past her constricted throat, Cole answered.

"We've determined that the best place to hide—"

"Silence!"

Amelia jumped. In the three days since this nightmare started, she'd never heard Chien Fou's voice raise above a murmur.

"I did not ask you, Cole."

"Yes, Leader."

Chien Fou gestured, and a guard moved to stand between Amelia and Cole. A second slid into place on Cole's other side.

Amelia's pulse thrummed in her temples as she sent Cole a silent message. *I can do it. Don't get into trouble.*

"Miss Hopkins, do you have the blueprints for me?"

"Sir, there's no need to make structural modifications. We've decided to put the C-4 in the starboard hold." Her pulse beat even faster—so fast it threatened to steal her breath. "We'll have to counterbalance it with lead on the port side, but using the hold will reduce the amount of work involved. This afternoon I discussed this with my ballast crew, without going into specifics. I put the supervisor in touch with your munitions expert. They should have the seven boats done by tomorrow afternoon. Then all you'll have to do is make sure the boats are positioned with the starboard side toward the tanker's most vulnerable point."

Dear heavens, she sounded like one of them. She clamped her lips shut but not before a small moan escaped.

"Miss Hopkins? Is something wrong?"

She laughed—an odd, unamused exclamation. "Is something wrong?" Beside her, even with a burly guard between them, she felt Cole stiffen.

But her fear was morphing into something else— frustration at the helplessness of her position. Anger at the amoral fiend sitting so calmly in front of her.

"I'm harboring of one of the most bitter enemies of

the United States in my home. I'm giving you the recipe for using my father's boats to cripple our country, and you ask me if there's something wrong?"

The guard beside her moved, and suddenly she felt the unmistakable circle of a gun barrel pressed into the side of her neck.

Chien Fou gave the guard a slight shake of his head and the pressure disappeared immediately.

"Regrettably for you, what you've just said is entirely true. If you want to remain safe, not to mention ensure your father's safety, you need to stay focused on your goal, which is modifying those boats. The sooner you're done with that, the sooner we'll be away from Raven's Cliff."

Amelia sniffed. "You're not going to take the chance that I or anyone else in this town might warn the government about what you're doing."

"If you do your job right, Miss Hopkins, your employees need never know that they were not a vital part of a U.S. effort to stop a terrorist attack."

"My employees are not idiots," she snapped, her anger rising. "Do you think my ballast crew doesn't know what we're putting into those boats? Even I know what C-4 is. There's no explanation that would satisfy them." The room was too small, too hot. Her ears were beginning to buzz and her vision was turning dark. She put a hand to her forehead. It felt damp.

Chien Fou frowned, the first time she'd ever seen anything other than a benign smile on his face. "Then I'd suggest you come up with a story that will. I don't want to waste the time or the manpower required to ensure the integrity of my plan, but I can assure you I'll do it if necessary."

She knew what that meant. He'd slaughter the entire town if he had to.

But she'd die if she had to, to save Raven's Cliff.

"If you kill another person—" Amelia took a step forward.

Pain burst across her cheek, blinding her. She swayed. Something warm and wet tickled her chin. When she touched her tongue to her lip, she tasted blood.

"Amelia!" Cole shouted.

She heard the sickening sound of something solid hitting flesh. A startled grunt from Cole. Another awful thud.

Then her arms were jerked behind her. It was the guard who'd backhanded her. His grip was brutal. Her muscles and joints screamed with strain.

Glancing sideways, she saw Cole doubled over. The guard who'd sucker-punched him jerked him upright and held a gun to his back. Cole's face was ashen.

"Guards, get this little drama under control." Chien Fou was clearly agitated, even frightened.

"Cole. You seem a little too concerned about Miss Hopkins's well-being."

Cole coughed, a strangled sound. Amelia dug her fingernails into the flesh of her palms to keep from looking at him. She couldn't let on that she was concerned about him. If Chien Fou knew she cared what happened to Cole, there was no telling what he might do.

"Perhaps this is a good time to mention what happened earlier today. Abel tells me he found you and Miss Hopkins in a compromising position—in public."

Cole didn't answer.

"Even more interesting is what he overheard. Did you really tell Miss Hopkins that you wished you could tell her who you really are?"

Amelia surreptitiously glanced his way. She couldn't read anything in his eyes. All she could see was the blood's trail down his temple to his jaw and the poorly disguised pain etched on his face.

He jerked against the guard's grip. Chien Fou waved a hand, and the guard let him go.

Cole doubled over again, his hand to his belly, where the guard had rammed him.

"You said do anything necessary," Cole rasped.

Anything necessary.

Anything necessary...

Anything—

The words echoed in Amelia's ears. Over and over again. For a split second, she couldn't make sense of them. She understood the words—each one separately— she just couldn't put them together. She shook her head, trying to shake off the fog and pain of the backhand to her face and the nauseating warmth of the room.

"That's true. I did tell you to do whatever it took to gain her cooperation. But I envisioned force more than seduction."

"I told you I'm not into rape," Cole muttered.

Those words she understood. Tears clogged her throat. She felt sick at heart. Cole had done what he'd been ordered to do. She supposed she should be thankful that rape wasn't his style.

She'd taken a chance. A foolish chance. She'd believed a man just because he'd promised her she could.

Cole's dark gaze held something she'd have interpreted as regret a few moments ago. Now it just looked like a pathetic plea for forgiveness.

She turned away in disgust. Straining against the guard's painful hold, she glared at Chien Fou. "Cooperation? You want my cooperation? After what you've just told me, I see no reason to cooperate with you. You're going to kill us anyway, and maybe I can slow if not stop your perverted mission."

Chien Fou's mouth quirked in that infamous smile. "Oh, Miss Hopkins. Can you really be so naive? You will cooperate with me. I have so many inducements at my disposal that it's hard to choose just one. In fact, now that I think about it, I don't have to choose one. I can use several. They will provide a nice check and balance system for me—and for you, so that you don't forget why you are cooperating."

Chien Fou had that deceptively benign look in his eye again. It was tinged with a deadly threat, and it made Amelia's blood run cold.

She shivered. "Tell this filthy terrorist to get his hands off me," she snapped.

Chien Fou waved his hand. The guard let go and stepped back. "As it happens," he said, "I've heard that your father is not just recovering from the flu. He's actually on medication for a heart condition."

Chien Fou sent an amused glance Cole's way before cocking his head in Amelia's direction. "Is that true?"

She froze, shock numbing her fingers and lips. Cole had betrayed her again? He'd told Chien Fou about her father's condition?

"At first I was irritated—if Reginald Hopkins was incapable of producing the innovative design techniques for which he's famous, what good was he to me? Then I realized I held the perfect leverage to make sure you did as you were told."

"What have you done to my father? Where is he?"

"I've removed him and the mayor to more secure if less luxurious accommodations."

"I have to see him—now. He needs me."

"No. Absolutely not. I'll take care of your father as long as you cooperate. Don't get any ideas of foolish bravery or he will suffer."

Amelia took a step forward. Immediately the guard grabbed her arm and the cold circle of steel was pressed to the side of her neck again.

"That includes talking back," Chien Fou finished.

He turned to Cole. "Your job is to make sure Miss Hopkins is kept in a meek and cooperative state. If you can't handle that job, I can assign someone to her who can."

Cole sent a glance in her direction before dropping his gaze to his boots. "I can handle it, Leader."

Chien Fou gestured to the guard at his left hand. The guard poured him a glass of water.

"By the way, Cole, you said you wished you could tell her who you really are. Why don't you do that now?"

Cole's shoulders straightened and he raised his head to meet Chien Fou's gaze. "What do you mean, Leader?"

"Oh, please, Cole. Surely you didn't think I would accept you into our organization without running a thorough background check."

"My background has nothing to do with my capabilities or my beliefs. You, of all people, should know that."

For a long moment the two men engaged in a silent battle of wills. The tension in the room rose as the guards became increasingly agitated.

Finally, Chien Fou turned to Amelia. "Meet Cole Robinson, only son of George Robinson, former congressman from the great state of Florida."

Robinson? Where had she heard about a Congressman Robinson?

Robinson! The answer slammed into her brain like a truck into the side of a building.

Congressman George Robinson—traitor. She remembered seeing his face on the national news, right before he held up a newspaper to hide from the flashing cameras.

"George Robinson was your father?" she asked, wishing he'd somehow deny it, disprove it.

But the truth was there in his emotionless stare. His father had sold secrets to enemies of the United States.

And Cole was following in his footsteps.

COLE STOOD perfectly still as Amelia was escorted out of Chien Fou's suite. He would have liked to have pretended that he was stoic in the face of Chien Fou's threats, but in truth his belly hurt so badly that if he moved he was afraid he'd throw up from the pain. And the damn room was too hot. It took all his concentration to stay upright.

Once Amelia was gone and the door to the suite was closed, Chien Fou made an infinitesimal gesture. The guard who'd sucker-punched Cole stuck the barrel of a big gun into his side.

When Cole didn't move, the guard prodded him

with the barrel. Whatever the butt of the gun had done to his insides, the barrel magnified. Sharp pain stabbed his side.

He stepped forward with all the dignity he could muster.

"Did you really think I didn't know about your father?"

Cole shrugged, forcing himself not to wince.

A flicker of Chien Fou's gaze warned him—too late.

The guard slammed the butt of the machine pistol into his lower back. He arched backward and a groan escaped his clenched jaws. He staggered, but kept his footing.

The terrorist leader didn't tolerate disrespect. Cole figured he'd better remember that or soon he wouldn't be able to walk.

"No, Leader. I knew you'd figure out that I'm his son."

"That's better, Cole. I really shouldn't have allowed you to think you were immune to discipline. Now, what I can't understand is why you didn't tell me about your father yourself."

Cole cringed, and wondered if he'd make it through the rest of the evening. Chien Fou's irrational bursts of temper were famous inside the GFF. He had no compunction about torturing and killing even the most competent member of his organization if they displeased him.

And Cole had displeased him in several ways.

He remembered the hopeless attitude with which he'd gone into this undercover operation. At the time, he'd figured if he didn't make it out alive, at least his life would have made up in part for what his father had done.

Now that the possibility of death was imminent,

though, he realized he wasn't quite as fatalistic as he'd been at the start of this mission. At some point within the last few days, Cole had stopped looking backward with regret and started looking forward—toward the future. With anticipation.

A movement by the guard at his side jump-started Cole's answer. "I was afraid to tell you, Leader."

The guard relaxed minutely.

Chien Fou sat up. "Afraid?"

Good. He'd caught the leader's attention.

"Afraid of what?"

"Of you, Leader. Of what you would think if you knew. I worried that you would doubt my sincerity— my devotion—to the cause."

Chien Fou laughed, a sinister sound. "Cole, my dear boy, of course I doubt you. Do you really think I got this far by trusting the people who work for me? Now, I'm very unhappy with Miss Hopkins's attitude. Perhaps I should assign her care to someone else."

Cole's mouth went dry. He had to play this cool or Chien Fou might take her away from him just for meanness.

"I can handle her. I mistakenly thought you were amused by her spirit."

"Perhaps at first. But not now. Now it is merely tedious. I've received information from my sources that the tankers will be here sooner than we thought. They are outrunning a storm in the north Atlantic, so instead of two weeks, we only have a week. No time to indulge her displays of silly courage or your adolescent flirtation." He picked up his water glass and took a sip. "We can't waste time. Break her."

Chien Fou's voice ripped through Cole's stoic demeanor. He clamped his jaw and forced himself not to react.

Break her. "Yes, Leader," he said as steadily as he could.

Chien Fou's gaze narrowed.

Cole knew his face was pale and clammy. He knew if he had to stay in this oppressively hot room for another two minutes, he'd pass out. He stood at attention, holding his breath, expecting a crushing blow to his kidneys or the back of his knees.

"You have feelings for her."

"No!" Cole bit his cheek. "No, Leader. I merely do not get my enjoyment from brutalizing women."

"Then I will find someone who—"

"No," he interrupted. "I'll do it. I'll take care of her."

Chien Fou looked down at his water glass, turning it in his hand.

Sweat trickled down the curve of Cole's back. He had orders not to compromise the operation, but there was no way in hell he could stand by while Amelia was brutalized. Somehow, he had to stop the terrorists and keep her safe at the same time.

"This is your last chance, Cole. Yours *and* hers. Neither one of you is irreplaceable."

COLE SLIPPED THROUGH the doors to Amelia's suite. To his relief, the lights were out and she was in bed. Hopefully asleep. He walked quietly across the room and dug into his duffel bag for his electric razor. Then he stepped out onto the balcony.

The cold air hit his damp skin and he shivered. For

a few seconds he gripped the steel railing and bowed his head, letting the chill in the air wipe away his nausea. If only it could do the same for the pain.

He felt his ribs with his fingertips. He hit a tender place on his right side. Bruised, as painful as hell, but not broken. He sighed in relief and winced.

He looked out over the town. Raven's Cliff was nestled in between the cliffs of the craggy Maine coastline, as its name suggested. It was the perfect place for the Global Freedom Front to locate their base. From this isolated little town they could mount their attack on supertankers up and down the Eastern Seaboard in almost perfect seclusion.

Cole glanced back toward Amelia's bed, although he knew the drapes were closed.

What would have happened if the GFF had chosen a different town, or if he hadn't managed to get into Chien Fou's good graces?

What if he'd never met Amelia?

Stop, damn it. He refused to let his thoughts continue down that path.

Carefully surveying the area around him to be sure no one was watching, he extracted the miniature satellite phone from the battery cavity of the electric shaver and pressed a preset number.

"Yes?"

The person on the other end didn't identify himself but Cole knew the voice. It was his handler, Patrick Hayes.

"Four-four-oh-three-two-nine-three," he said. He saw movement down below, on the docks in front of Hopkins Boatworks. He watched two men walk out to the end of a pier. A light flared, then died.

Cigarettes. Either guards or Hopkins employees, taking a break.

"Confirmed," the voice finally said.

"Reports indicate the delivery date has been moved up. True?"

"Confirmed."

"Time frame?"

"Five days."

Damn. Less time than he'd hoped for.

"Are you ready for delivery?"

"Negative," Cole answered. "Working on it."

"What's wrong?" Patrick had relaxed a bit. Still, Cole knew he only had a few seconds left before his friend/superior cut the connection.

"Besides the innocents involved? He knows who I am." Cole stepped over to the far side of the balcony. "He suspects my motives."

"Do you need extracting?"

"No! I can't leave here until I'm sure these people are safe. There's no way I'm going to leave Amelia in the hands of these terrorist bastards."

"Amelia?"

Damn it. "Amelia Hopkins. The boatbuilder's daughter."

"I see. Can you handle the new timetable?"

"No problem."

He turned to head back toward the balcony door, and found himself less than five feet away from the boatbuilder's daughter herself. Her eyes were wide as saucers and glittering in the lights that shone from the boatyard.

"I have to go," he said shortly.

"The mission is the priority."

Cole knew that if he didn't answer Patrick with the correct phrase, a Homeland Security helicopter would be headed toward Raven's Cliff within ninety seconds.

"The priority is the mission," he recited—the code phrase for *all clear.* Then, without taking his eyes off her, he said, "Out."

He hung up and slid the phone into the pocket of his slacks. He swallowed.

She lifted her chin.

"I thought you were asleep," he said, forcing himself to hold her gaze.

"Who was that?"

She rubbed her arms, and Cole's eyes flew to the tips of her breasts, clearly outlined by the satiny material of her navy blue pajamas. She probably thought they were modest. But they weren't. Not from where he stood.

"Get inside. You're freezing."

Amelia met his gaze, then looked down at herself. She disappeared through the balcony door.

Cole took a deep breath of cold September air, fitted the tiny phone back inside the shaver and went inside.

Amelia had put on a negligee. It was long-sleeved, but it tied just under her breasts and negated any pretense at modesty.

"Who were you talking to?"

"How much did you hear?"

She flung out her hands. "Are you going to answer every question with another question? I heard enough to make me very confused."

Cole didn't know whether to be relieved or worried. She was extremely smart and highly intuitive. And he could tell by the way she was watching him that her brain was whirring with the implications of what she'd heard.

"Look, Amelia, I need you to trust me."

"And I need a reason. I need you to tell me what's really going on here. Just who are you, Cole Robinson?"

Chapter Nine

Who are you? As soon as the question left her lips, Amelia saw the answer on Cole's face. His already strained expression turned panicky.

"It's true, isn't it? Your father is George Robinson?"

His back stiffened. Then he turned away and bent down to stuff the modified shaver into his duffel bag. When he did, an almost silent groan escaped his lips.

He was hurt.

No. Stop it. Her rational brain won out over her totally irrational heart—at least for now.

"I can't do this anymore," she said as forcefully as she could. "This nightmare has got to end. I don't care how at this point."

Cole rose, his hand pressed to his side. "Amelia—"

"No." She held up her hands. "Don't even try it. You ask me to trust you one more time and I'll—" She paused for an instant.

"I don't know what I'll do. But I'll tell you this right now. I'd rather die than help that madman." Suddenly her pulse hammered in her ears and her breaths came in short puffs through her constricted throat. She realized she meant it. No way were she or her father going to make it through this alive. So why help the enemy accomplish their goal?

"I'd rather die."

Before she even registered that he'd moved, he was in front of her, so close she could feel his heat. "Amelia, listen to me. Don't give up on me now. If you can just be brave for a little while longer—"

"*Brave?* It's not bravery to help a terrorist betray my country."

"Please, Amelia. If I could—"

"If you could what?" She knew she was very close to hysteria but she didn't care. "Finish one of your mysterious sentences? You keep on begging me to trust you, to hold on just a little longer. Why? What are you waiting for?"

She brushed her hair back from her face with both hands. "Tell me one reason why I shouldn't just confront your *leader* and goad him into shooting me. It wouldn't take much."

That tidbit of his telephone conversation she'd overheard came back to her. "Who were you talking to out there anyhow? Chien Fou's superior? An inside person in Raven's Cliff?" An ironic laugh bubbled up from her chest. "A supersecret anonymous government antiterrorist agency?"

His expression changed to one of disbelief and he swallowed. He stepped closer.

Her instinctive reaction was to recoil, but he touched her arms. His touch was a caress, gentle and protective.

"You're close," he whispered, staring intently into her eyes.

Amelia couldn't gauge his expression. "I'm close?"

"I took an oath. I swore on my life that I would keep this mission secret. Your life, the lives of everyone in this town depend on me keeping that oath."

"Cole? What are you saying?"

"I'm with Homeland Security. The truth is what I told you and your employees. It's Chien Fou and his Global Freedom Front that I've been lying to."

Amelia's head swam. Cole's words circled around her as somewhere—maybe in her mind—a voice whispered, *Trust him.*

"So you really are with Homeland Security? And the terrorists think you're on their side?" Her lips felt numb. Her *brain* felt numb. The words she'd just said were unbelievable.

Trust him.

"So all that stuff you spouted to my employees, all that *supersecret government plot* is true?"

He nodded solemnly.

But she still couldn't quite wrap her brain around the concept.

"So why are we loading pounds of C-4 into the boats? And mapping the paths of the tankers? You know what Chien Fou is planning. Why hasn't Homeland Security stopped them?"

"It's not about proof. We've got plenty of proof. We've got recordings of Chien Fou claiming responsibility for explosions that murdered dozens of military personnel and civilians. What we need is a controlled environment where we can move in and capture Chien Fou and the major players in the Global Freedom Front."

"You're going to do that here?"

"No. Too many civilians around. Chien Fou is a narcissist. He wants to see the destruction he's caused. He'll be on a boat at a safe distance with his guards, waiting and watching for the explosions to start."

Amelia rubbed her arms and shivered. But the chill that slithered through her wasn't from the temperature outside. It was from within. "*Will* the explosions start?"

"Yep. Right on time. Chien Fou has a small crew of electricians who will affix detonators to the C-4. The detonators will be set off remotely, using cell phones. And that's where you and I come in. We need to snip the wires inside the detonators. It will have to be done at the last possible second, at a point where Leader and his guards have already left in their boat—or are about to. After the last inspection."

"What if something goes wrong?"

"Nothing's going to go wrong. Trust me."

And there it was again. That thing that hung between them like a shield. *Trust.*

"Do you trust me, Amelia?"

Cole watched Amelia's face. He knew by looking at her what she was going through. Her expression mirrored her feelings as they churned and morphed inside her. She'd gone from shock to disbelief to doubt to uncertainty.

And that's where she was right now. She wasn't sure if she could believe him, much less trust him.

He understood perfectly. She could end up as an accessory to treason. Or could end up dead. It all depended on whether he was telling the truth.

The decision was in her hands. He'd given her everything he could, but only she could decide what to do.

"I don't have a choice, do I?"

"You always have a choice."

She shook her head. "Then I have to trust you, because I can't believe the alternative."

"Good. That's great." He couldn't believe the weight that lifted from his shoulders. "Because we've got a lot of work to do before morning. There's something else we need to do. And it won't be easy. I have to ask you to trust me one more time."

She shot him an ironic look. "You think the last time was easy? I'll trust you, Cole Robinson. What other choice do I have?"

He nodded. That was the spot he was in, too. He had no choice, either. He had to trust her.

"Okay then. Where's that case of stage makeup you had with you the other night?"

IT WAS THREE DAYS later before Amelia saw Chien Fou again. She hadn't seen much of Cole, either. He came into her room after midnight and left before her alarm clock went off at seven.

She knew because when he eased onto the edge of her bed with a tired sigh, it woke her. She woke when he slipped out of bed in the morning to shower and shave, too.

In between, while he lay two feet away from her on her king-size bed, she felt safer and slept better than she ever had in her life.

In bed with a terrorist. Or a government spy. She didn't know.

When the guard who'd fetched her from the warehouse where she was inspecting the seven boats escorted her to Chien Fou's suite, Cole was there.

He didn't look at her, merely stood at ease and eyes forward in military fashion.

Which was good, because the charade she'd been playing for the past three days was about to be put to the ultimate test. Would stage makeup and her acting ability be enough to fool Chien Fou?

"Ah, Miss Hopkins."

She'd spent the past days avoiding people's gazes and acting like a victim. The makeup on her cheek and chin and above her eye itched and pulled her skin tight. She'd made up corpses and zombies and men after fist-fights before—for theater—back in college and here in Raven's Cliff.

But this was not a play. It was real life. And as Cole had explained to her two nights ago, her life and the lives of the people of Raven's Cliff depended on her acting ability. Chien Fou and his minions had to believe that Cole had subdued her by force.

"Miss Hopkins? Please step closer."

She stiffened. Cole had assured her that Chien Fou wouldn't inspect her too closely.

He's got a phobia about germs. I don't know how he got into a position of such power. Certainly not by brute force.

She took a small step closer, still not looking up. It galled her to act subservient in front of the slimy terrorist leader, but this was not about her pride. It was about protecting the people of Raven's Cliff and foiling a terrorist plot.

"Look at me, Miss Hopkins."

She felt Cole's silent encouragement, although he didn't move.

She raised her gaze to Chien Fou's.

He scrutinized her for a few seconds, frowning. "What happened to you?" he asked.

She let her gaze falter. "Nothing, sir."

"Miss Hopkins. Look at me and tell me what happened to you."

She feigned a glance toward Cole, then looked straight at Chien Fou. It wasn't hard to conjure up tears. All she had to do was to think about her father, poor Ross Fancher and his younger brother, Joey, not to mention the other people who would suffer if this maniac completed his plan.

She wrapped her arms around herself. "I...can't say."

"My dear girl. It's obvious that Cole has hurt you. Let me assign you to a different guard."

Amelia's gut clenched and her heart crashed against her chest wall. "No!" she blurted without thinking. "No, please. Not another—"

She bit off the words and stood stiffly, waiting to see what Chien Fou would do. Had her horrified outburst ruined the charade?

But he laughed. "Better the devil you know?" He waved a hand at her. "Back up."

She took a step back.

"Farther. Now tell me, do you feel the boats are ready?"

Dropping her gaze again, she nodded. "Yes, sir. The ballast is secured. All that's left now is to place the detonators and hook up the remote-control steering."

"Excellent. We launch tomorrow night. In less than forty-eight hours, the Eastern Seaboard of the United States will be permanently crippled."

AMELIA DIDN'T SEE Cole for the rest of the day, but just before dinner, Mrs. Winston asked her to come into the kitchen to taste the soup.

"It's your favorite," she said, "and I want you to taste it to be sure there's enough garlic."

In the kitchen, Mrs. Winston held a spoon for Amelia to taste. When she leaned forward to taste, Mrs. Winston whispered in her ear.

"Go to your suite right after dinner. Cole will meet you there."

Amelia looked up in surprise. "You're carrying messages for the enemy now?"

Mrs. Winston shook her head. "He's not the enemy. I can't say anything more, but you need to trust him."

Amelia laughed quietly. "You sound like the fortune-teller."

"What fortune-teller?"

"Never mind."

The door to the dining room swung open. It was one of Chien Fou's personal bodyguards.

"Is his dinner ready yet?" the man asked.

Mrs. Winston scowled. "Yes. Here you go. Meat with no sauce. Lettuce with no dressing. Hot water."

The guard took the tray and turned toward the door.

"Everybody else better get up here. I'm putting the food on the table now," she said as he left.

She turned toward Amelia. "I don't know why that leader bothers eating at all."

"I think he's worried that someone is going to poison him."

"Ha," Mrs. Winston said. "If I wanted to poison him, the absence of a sauce wouldn't stop me."

"Shh." Amelia chuckled. "Don't say that. You have no idea how ruthless Chien Fou is."

"Chien Fou? What the heck kind of a name is that?"

"A crazy one. By the way, the soup's perfect, as usual."

"Good."

After dinner, Amelia went to her suite. It was only seven-thirty, and she felt sure Cole wouldn't get there until much later. So she took a shower.

When she came out, dressed in nothing but a terry-cloth robe, she saw Cole out on the balcony, talking on his phone. She stopped. She'd never had a chance to study him, so she stood perfectly still. He leaned on the rail, dressed in old, faded jeans and a dark pullover shirt.

As she watched, he raised his head to look out toward the lighthouse, and his coiled grace and aristocratic profile made her throat ache. His chiseled features and toned body were incredibly beautiful.

But the picture of male perfection wasn't what got to her. Something in the tilt of his chin and the slope of his shoulders touched her heart. He seemed burdened. Lonely. Brave.

He nodded and turned his back to the sliding doors. Then he switched the phone to his other hand and rubbed the back of his neck.

He was hearing something he didn't like.

Amelia was dying to slide open the doors and eavesdrop, but she knew he would never make the same mistake twice. There was no way she'd have a chance in hell of sneaking up on him again.

So she grabbed her clothes and headed back into the bathroom. Behind her, she heard the almost-silent swish of the drapes.

"Amelia."

She had to admit she was beginning to like the way he drew out her name. *Ah-mee-lee-yah.* She turned, conscious of the fact that she was dressed in nothing but the robe, and it was slipping. She wanted to tighten the sash at her waist, but to do it she'd have to drop the clothes she held.

Cole's eyes took in her wet hair, the robe that was fast coming undone and her bare feet. His scrutiny felt like fingers sliding over her skin.

She shivered, as the tingle of awareness slithered all the way from her head to her feet. Her breasts tightened and scraped against the terry cloth.

With one hand she pulled the collar of the robe together.

"Have you got black pants and a black long-sleeved top?"

She blinked. "Yes. Why?"

"We need to get some sleep, because in a few hours, we're going to sneak down to the warehouse and disable the detonators."

"*We* are?"

He nodded. "Get dressed—in black, and then we'll try to sleep until 2:00 a.m. or so."

She put down the clothes, tightened the robe and dug in her closet for black jeans and a black turtleneck sweater. Then she headed into the bathroom to dress.

When she came out, Cole had donned the black wool pants and black pullover he'd worn the first time she'd seen him. He looked tall and handsome and confident.

"Lie down."

"Just exactly what are we going to do?"

"I'll tell you. Lie down."

He stepped over to his side of the bed and stretched out on top of the covers.

Wondering what he was up to, Amelia turned out the bathroom light and walked around the bed. She gingerly lay on top of the covers on her side of the bed.

"Okay. I'm lying down. What next? Now are you going to command me to go to sleep?"

"Would it work?"

She shrugged in the darkness.

"We need a way to get out of the house without anyone knowing."

Amelia thought about the trapdoor her father had built into the bottom floor of the house. It led to a storm cellar set up inside a nearby cave.

"There's a trapdoor with a rope ladder, but it's been years since I used it."

"Trap door? I studied your father's surveillance setup and I didn't see a trapdoor."

"There's no camera there. I used it to sneak out when Dad was asleep."

He grunted quietly. "Is that the only exit without surveillance?"

She nodded.

"Okay, then. We climb down the rope ladder. What's down there?"

"Cliffs. There's an old storm cellar built into the side of the cliffs but it hasn't been used in ages, either."

Amelia shivered. "There are probably all kinds of bugs and varmints in there."

"I want to see it. It could come in handy. Is it hidden?"

"I never thought about it, but yes, I think you could say it's hidden."

"Good. Do we need to go through it to get down to the docks?"

"No. We can pick up the path right below the trapdoor."

"And the path goes all the way down to the dock?"

"Yes."

He made a satisfied sound, then took a deep breath and yawned. "Get some sleep. I'll wake you."

Chapter Ten

Cole opened his eyes and checked his watch about three seconds before its alarm went off. He turned off the alarm and looked across the expanse of snowy-white sheets. Amelia lay on her side, her face relaxed, her lips slightly open. His gaze traced the makeup that simulated bruises on her cheek and chin and the fake cut she'd applied to her forehead just above her brow.

The sight of them—even knowing they were fake—made his stomach churn. He was disgusted by what everyone thought he'd done to her. He'd done a lot of things he wasn't proud of during his time undercover with the Global Freedom Front, but he'd never killed anyone and he'd never hurt a woman.

The fact that he hadn't really hurt her didn't help as much as he'd expected it to. He still felt guilty, sullied. As soon as all this mess was over, he wanted to take her and hold her and try to explain to her about the things he'd had to do, and why he'd had to allow Chien Fou and his minions to think she'd been beaten and brutalized.

"Amelia?" he said softly.

She whispered something in her sleep. He could see her eyelids fluttering. She was dreaming.

He put a hand on her shoulder. "Amelia?"

Her eyes flew open.

"Hey, it's me. Cole. Time to wake up."

She blinked and moistened her lips. The sight of her tongue sent his libido rocketing into outer space.

Get over it, he ordered his body. He was on a life-and-death mission. No time for inconvenient urges or emotions.

He sat up. "Let's go. We don't have much time."

He pulled on heavy-duty climbing boots. "Have you got climbing boots?" he asked as he laced them.

"Of course," she said. Her voice was husky with sleep. It was the sexiest sound he'd ever heard.

"Any gear?"

"Come on, Robinson. The cliff isn't that steep. It's a difficult walk, not a climb."

"All right, then. How do we get to that trapdoor?"

"Lucky for you, it's easy. You see, when Dad built this house, his primary concern was for me. So he put the door leading down to the storm cellar in my closet."

Cole turned to stare at her. "Why didn't you tell me that?"

"I just did."

"I should have known that from the very beginning."

"Why? You weren't planning on using it until now."

He glared at her. "What if something had happened? What if we'd needed to escape the house?"

"Then I'd have told you."

He wanted to shake her. He wanted to yell at her about the importance of knowing all the escape routes from any location. But time was wasting, and she was right. He knew now.

Later, after all this was over, he promised himself. Later he'd explain the concept of *complete information* to her.

If they were lucky enough to get to *later* alive.

"Okay," he said tightly. "Got your boots on? Come into the bathroom."

"Why?"

"Because I said to." He glared at her. "This is how it's going to work. I'm the boss. You do what I say—without question. Got it?"

Amelia's chin went up, but to her credit, she nodded. "Yes, sir." She walked past him into the bathroom.

He followed and closed the door. Then he took a small metal tin out of his pocket and opened it.

"What's that?"

"It's camouflage face paint. It'll help keep us from being seen in the dark. Sit."

She sat on the vanity bench and lifted her face.

Her trust in him was sobering. He'd asked her to trust him, but he hadn't let himself expect her to. Given the same circumstances, he wouldn't have.

He opened the tin and spread the greasy paste across her cheekbones, forehead, nose and chin, mixing the colors for maximum light absorption. Then he spread it down her neck until it touched the edge of her turtleneck.

She kept her eyes closed while he worked.

"Okay, You're done."

She touched a fingertip to her cheek, then looked at it. "Green and brown?"

"Like I said, it's camo. I don't have black."

She stood and looked in the mirror, contorting her mouth. "It's sticky."

"It'll dry." He smeared his face and neck with the gunk, then washed his hands.

"We look like special forces, don't we?"

He met her gaze in the mirror. "*I* look like special forces. You look like a little girl playing dress-up."

"What? There aren't any female special forces?"

"Nope. Not that I know of."

"So I'll be the first."

"Just follow my orders."

She stuck her tongue out at him.

He suppressed the urge to smile. He'd give anything to be in a situation where they could laugh about what they were about to do, but it was deadly serious.

"We need to go. Show me the trapdoor."

She went over to the closet and pulled up a section of carpet. Sure enough, there was a small rectangle in the floor with a pull ring inset into it. He lifted the ring and pulled.

The door hinged open without a sound. Just below the door was a large hook on which the rope ladder hung. It looked old, but it was made of nylon, so hopefully it was still capable of holding weight.

"You go ahead."

She nodded. "If you close the door until it's almost shut, then reach out and pull the carpet this way, it'll fall almost perfectly over the door when you let it close."

He cocked a brow at her. "Sneaked out some?"

She gave him a rueful smile that made her honey-colored eyes sparkle. "A few times."

"Nice." He bent and unhooked the ladder and let it fall. Then gestured with his head. "Go on."

"Don't I get a weapon?"

"No."

She started to say something else, but he leveled a gaze at her that had shut up big mean men. She nodded and lowered herself down the ladder.

When he was sure she was safely on the ground, he started down. He wasn't sure the rope would hold his greater weight, but the drop didn't look as if it was that far. About twenty feet or so. Not fun, but not the farthest he'd ever dropped in free fall.

When he got to the bottom, Amelia had her hands on a straight length of rope. As soon as he let go of the ladder, she started hauling the rope. The ladder rolled up and nestled in the frame of the trap door.

"So that rope hangs down all the time?"

She nodded. "It kind of looks like it was left over from something." She pointed to the end of the rope. "See how ragged it is? It's always looked that way."

"Your dad is a smart man."

She didn't answer.

They made their way down the cliff side without incident.

When they got to the dock, Cole put out a hand to stop her. "There are GFF guards around here. They patrol all night. We've got to be careful. If we're seen, we're toast. You stay here, in the shadow of this piling. I'm going up closer to the warehouse to see if I see any guards."

"Wait a minute," Amelia said, her pulse thrumming in her ears. She'd done okay so far, but Cole's wry remark about being toast reminded her of just how dangerous this venture was. "You're just going to stroll up there? What if someone sees you? What if you do run into a guard? He'll kill you. Why don't you carry a gun?"

"How do you know I don't?"

She gaped at him. "You're armed?"

He was crouched in front of her, his hand still out in a protective gesture, resting against her shoulder.

She swallowed as she studied the curve of his back, his lean waist and the pockets of his black wool pants. No bulges there—at least none she could see from the back.

She felt her face heat up at the thought of bulges. She shook her head, ridding herself of *those* kinds of thoughts. Getting distracted could get them killed.

He shifted and his powerful thighs strained the material of his pants as he crouched. His climbing boots were ankle-high and heavy duty. They could hide a lot more than a snug pullover or form-fitting wool pants could.

"Your ankle," she guessed, desperately pulling her gaze away from his thighs. "It's hidden in your boot, or in an ankle holster."

"Very good. See, my job is to be the nerdy guy. The one who figures out how to fix the boats to explode. So it wouldn't make sense for me to wear one of those bulky suits or hide a monstrous gun."

"Great. So if you run into one of the guards, you'll just shoot him? And what, throw the body into the water and claim the sound was a car backfiring?"

"If it comes to that. Now stay here. If I'm not back in five minutes, go back up to your room and tell whoever asks that you never saw me last night."

"I can't do that."

He twisted to face her, grabbing her upper arms. His thighs pressed against hers. "Listen to me, Amelia. Do you want to die? Because if you don't do exactly as I say, that's what's going to happen. I can't keep you safe if I can't depend on you do follow my orders *exactly*. Do you understand?"

She nodded, doing her best not to grimace at the pressure of his fingers on her flesh. He didn't know how hard he was squeezing.

"Hell." He let go. "I'm sorry." He touched her arm lightly. "Did I hurt you?"

"No. It's okay," she said quickly. "I understand."

He met her gaze for an instant, his jaw working. Then he nodded.

"Stay here."

When he rose and took off toward the warehouse, her breath caught in a very real fear that he wouldn't make it back alive. And the idea of him dying took her breath away. Like a sudden yet unyielding pain.

From somewhere the sound of voices reached her ears. She hunched her shoulders, making herself as small as she possibly could and held her breath. Her pulse pounded in her ears, drowning out all other sound.

Calm down. Breathe slow and steady. She had to hear whoever was approaching. Her life—and Cole's—depended on it.

She had to help him. Whether he was an undercover government agent or a ruthless terrorist, he was still the only person she could trust.

She counted her breaths, concentrating on slowing her pulse.

She heard the voices again, this time much closer. There was no place to hide, other than the piling she was crouched behind. There was no moon tonight, but floodlights cast enough light to see by. No way she'd be invisible, even wearing black.

Where was Cole? Was he safe? Hidden? Surely she'd have heard shouts or a scuffle—or a gunshot—if they'd spotted him.

The crunch of boots on gravel came from somewhere too close behind her. *The guards!* Her shoulders tensed and all her strength went into staying still.

"—wiped out. I'd like to be home in my own bed."

"Yeah, well, hang in there. As soon as the attack is over, the Leader's going to want to go underground for a few months."

"I don't know. I heard somebody say he's already planning a similar attack on the West Coast."

"Yeah?"

The guard said something else but it was drowned out by the crunch of their footsteps.

Amelia breathed a tentative sigh of relief. They'd passed by without seeing her—this time. But she didn't dare move. Her left leg was asleep and she had a cramp in her right calf that was about to make her topple over. She closed her eyes and tried to pretend she wasn't hurting.

Another sound reached her ears. *Be invisible.* She held her breath.

A shadow loomed over her and she was blanketed by a strong, hot body and warm breaths whispered across her cheek.

"Shh. It's me."

Cole.

For a few seconds she gave in to the wonderful feeling of his body curled around her. Then he rolled and twisted until he was sitting with his back against the piling and she was propped on his lap.

"I saw the guards. You did good. Are you okay?"

His whispers slithered through her like fingers of sexual pleasure caressing all her erogenous zones, including a couple of places she hadn't known could feel like that.

Like the skin of her temple. And the little bumps on her spine, which was pressed against the hot, hard front of his body.

She nodded.

She knew what he was doing. He was making sure they both fit into the shadow cast by the piling. It was a big post, but not big enough to hide them if they sat side by side.

He held her there, unmoving, his mouth close to her ear, his body curled around hers so intimately that she could feel the hardness of his erection pressed against her hip.

Dear heavens, he was turned on. Was it by her? By the danger? Both?

Not that it mattered. All that mattered to her at that moment was that she was turned on, too. Strangely, she had no idea why. Maybe it was the relief of not being spotted by the guards, coupled with Cole's protective, sensual closeness.

Just physical closeness. That was all.

Danger and a very hot, very sexy undercover agent. A thrill shuddered through her.

Cole went totally still, his erection still pressed against her.

She twisted slightly, enough to look at him.

A quiet groan escaped his lips and he grimaced. "Please be still," he hissed.

"I was so worried that the guards would see you."

He cupped her cheek in his hand and pressed his lips against her forehead. "They didn't. It's okay. We're okay, for now."

"Cole, I heard one of the guards say Chien Fou is planning another attack—this time on the West Coast."

"I know. Don't worry. We're going to stop him before he can do that."

She nodded. Whenever he spoke to her with that low, slightly raspy voice, she believed him. It was like a Pavlovian response.

He spoke. She believed.

"Just stay still. You're killing me when you move." His mouth and breath on her skin sent desire racing through her like a shot of adrenaline. A nearly silent whimper of longing escaped her lips, and she raised her head.

Cole made a sound, deep in his throat. Then he accepted her invitation. He kissed her—deeply, thoroughly. She tasted the waxy camo makeup they wore. It blended with the taste of him—dark, sweet and spicy, like bitter chocolate. His erection pulsed against her, stirring her own need.

Gingerly, slowly, his hands tightened. He lifted her and turned her toward him. Then he kissed her again.

His tongue and lips worked magic, drawing her to him like a moth to a candle, coaxing her closer to his dangerous heat.

But of all she'd been through in the past three days, kissing Cole Robinson felt like the least dangerous thing she'd done. She wrapped her hands around his neck and opened to him.

He probed and nipped, giving her his breath as he took hers. His hands slid from her shoulders to her waist.

Then he froze.

Amelia stopped. "What is it?" she whispered. "Did you hear something?"

"This is stupid," he muttered, furtively glancing around. His comment wasn't meant to be a personal slight. But still it hurt. Hurt in a way she'd never experienced before. And that was a bad sign.

She knew he was right. Agreed, even. She should have stopped it before it got started.

"Very stupid," she said shortly, wincing as her cramping, tingling legs pulled her back to reality. She'd like to move, to escape the heat of his hard, aroused body. Get the waxy, chocolate scent of him out of her nostrils and his kisses out of her head. But the piling hadn't gotten any bigger, and they were skirting the edges of the shadow already.

She gritted her teeth and tried to act as if she wasn't sitting on his lap. "What did you see? Where are the guards?"

He cleared his throat. "There are six on foot and two anchored out in a boat just beyond that second buoy." He pointed. "The six are walking in pairs, and trying to cover all three sides of the boatyard all the time. But—"

"But the whole thing is too big for them."

Cole nodded. "As soon as those two guards pass us

again, which will probably be in about fifteen minutes, we can maneuver around the landlocked side of the dock and make our way to the warehouse where the loaded boats are." He paused. "Unless you know a secret way to get there."

She closed her eyes and thought about the layout of the boatyard. "No. Nothing that's better than what you said."

"Okay. So we've got about fifteen minutes." He looked at her from under his brow. "Got anything you want to do?"

She bit her lip and hoped she wasn't turning red. Not that he could see if she was. "I'd like to straighten my legs."

"Here." He lifted her and set her down between his legs.

She frowned. "You're kidding, right?"

"Not at all. Sit here and stretch your legs out in line with the piling's shadow."

She pushed back until her behind touched his front. He was still aroused. She suppressed a moan. At the same time he drew in a sharp breath.

"Are you sure you want to be this self-sacrificing?" she teased.

"Shut up."

She leaned back against him and slowly straightened her legs. The cramp in the right leg eased, but when she moved her left leg it screamed in pin-pricked agony as the circulation returned.

Her hands, resting on his thighs, curled and she dug her fingernails in, trying not to cry out.

"Hey!" he muttered.

"Sorry. My leg's asleep."

"Try digging into *your* thigh, not mine, to wake it up." His words were sarcastic, but he wrapped his arms around her, his hands on her middle.

After a few seconds, she rested her head against his shoulder. The pressure of his erection was solid, unyielding. His breaths were fast but steady, and his chest rose and fell rhythmically.

She'd never been surrounded by a man, not like this. Her experience had mostly been gathered in college, with boys, not men.

Since she'd returned to Raven's Cliff, she hadn't dated much. And she'd never had a man in her bed overnight.

Ever. Until Cole.

There were so many things about him that were different than anything she'd ever been exposed to. Not the least of which was the question of who he really was—undercover agent or terrorist.

As soon as that thought entered her head, it was followed by another, more disturbing one.

Could she be falling in love with a man who was an enemy of the United States of America?

Chapter Eleven

After the guards walked by again on their rounds, Cole instructed Amelia to stay in his shadow as they sneaked toward the warehouse.

He crept from one piling to another, until they were at the end of the dock. A gravel parking area stretched before them, lit by the boatyard floodlights.

He'd already gauged the distance and their level of exposure. He knew that the two guards anchored out in the bay couldn't see them.

He put his arm around Amelia's shoulders and whispered in her ear. "The guards on the south side aren't a problem. The ones on this side are at the far end right now, but the west-side guards are close. I need you to run as fast as you can. Stop when you're in the shadows of the warehouse and wait for me."

"Why—"

He squeezed her shoulders. "What did I tell you? I'm the boss."

She looked up at him and he saw her throat move as she swallowed.

He kissed her temple and pressed his cheek against

hers for a nanosecond. "Trust me. If something happens and I don't make it across the parking lot—"

She stiffened.

"Hey, soldier," he growled. "Snap to it. This is war. If I don't make it, you scream bloody murder and tell whoever finds you that I forced you to come with me."

He felt her head shaking no.

"This is not a negotiation. Do you understand?"

"Yes, sir," she whispered almost silently.

"Okay. I'm going to count to three. On three, you run. I promise I'll be right behind you."

"Cole—?"

"One," he whispered forcefully. "Two—" He took his arm away from her shoulders as he felt her tense in preparation for running. He placed a hand in the middle of her back and applied a steady pressure.

"Three!" He pushed.

She shot out of the shadows and ran, her legs and arms pumping like a sprinter's as she kicked up gravel with her heavy climbing boots.

He slipped his SIG out of his boot, pressed his shoulder against the shadowed side of the piling to steady himself and aimed at her back.

Holding his breath, he waited. There was no way the guards couldn't hear the gravel crunching. The question was, would they investigate? He'd heard them talking about their boring, exhausting night-guard duty. Maybe they wouldn't bother.

Yeah. And maybe pigs would fly.

He leaned out a little farther, watching Amelia's progress, alert to any movement or sound.

She melted into the shadows.

Cole released the breath he hadn't realized he was holding. She'd made it.

He tensed, listening, but the night was quiet. The only sound was the sloshing of waves against the rocks and an occasional call of a nocturnal bird.

He surveyed the parking lot. He'd already worked out a path that would make the least noise—for himself. He hadn't even tried to explain the circuitous route to Amelia. She'd have been too concerned about staying on the path. It would have made her too slow.

He took a deep breath and headed across, hoping like hell that the guards had dismissed the noise, or had been talking and not heard it.

Amelia pressed her back against the cold metal of the warehouse wall and waited. She didn't hear anything. Nothing. No boots crunching on gravel, no guards yelling.

What was Cole doing? She tried to rationalize an answer. He'd gone a different way. He was waiting until the coast was clear.

She counted off the seconds, until she lost count. How many minutes had gone by? Her back was getting cold and her pulse was pounding like a jackhammer in her head.

How long was she supposed to wait before she decided he'd been captured? Her imagination fed her all sorts of horrific possibilities. What if the terrorists had some super-fancy silent weapon, and Cole was already dead?

What if they'd captured him and were taking him someplace to torture and kill him?

Each random thought ratcheted up her panic until she felt like screaming.

"Okay, soldier," she whispered to herself. "It's up to you. No time to panic." She had to get into the warehouse and disable those detonators by herself.

Without Cole.

Her eyes stung and her panic grew. How would she bear it if he was dead?

A faint sound reached her ears. The soft thud of a footstep.

At the same time, the wall vibrated against her back. Her senses suddenly hyperalert, she glanced in the direction of the sound, tensed and ready to run if she had to.

A shadow, darker than the others, moved toward her.

She straightened and took a step backward, away from the advancing shadow.

"Hey, Amelia." The words were barely even a whisper. "We made it."

"Cole!" Her breath rushed out in a sigh of relief. "How did you do that without making a sound?"

"Shh. No time." He felt for her hand. "We've got to get inside."

"There's an emergency entrance on the south side. I can disable the alarm system."

"Lead the way."

She led Cole around the building to a small, nondescript door. She bent and dug around in the dirt piled against the wall. After a few seconds her fingers closed around a small metal box. It felt warm.

She breathed a sigh of relief. She brushed away the dirt from around it. When she opened the metal lid, a faint blue glow lit the digital number pad. She entered the code.

After a couple of seconds, a faint whir told her the code had worked. She closed the box and stuck it back in the dirt, then pushed open the warehouse door.

Cole stopped her with a hand on her arm. "What happens when we open this door to leave?"

"I've turned off the alarm. I'll need to reset it once we're out."

He nodded, then stepped through the door, sweeping the area with his weapon. She slipped in behind him and closed the door.

"Damn, it's darker than the inside of a black cat in here," he whispered. "Hang on."

She heard him digging in his pockets.

"I've got a glow light. It's good for about a half hour."

"That'll be plenty to light the way to a toolbox. There's a wind-up flashlight in each box."

She heard a thump and light flared. Cole's camouflaged face looked eerie in the faint light. "Where are the toolboxes?"

"Right here." She took the glow light from him. "There's a smaller toolbox on each boat, too. Contains the basics."

In front of each boat was a wooden crate with a hinged lid. She lifted the lid. "Here's the wind-up flashlight." She pressed a metal cylinder into his hand. "And here are some wire cutters, too."

"Great. Grab 'em. I've got one pair, but a backup never hurts."

They climbed up into the first boat.

"The detonators should be in the same place on each boat, right?" Amelia asked.

Cole nodded. "Usually it's attached to a blasting cap that's placed right on the C-4. When the signal is sent to the detonator cord, the electrical charge blows the blasting cap, which in turn sets off the C-4." He shone the flashlight down into the starboard hold.

"There it is."

Amelia held the flashlight while Cole examined the wires.

"Good. Right here, where the detonator cord is attached to the blasting cap, there's a snap-on cover. We can snip the wires, then close the cover and it will pass anything less than a detailed inspection."

"Show me exactly where to snip and I'll do some of the boats."

"No." She heard the plastic cover snap closed. Cole straightened. "You're staying with me. There are only seven boats. It won't take long."

"But with me working, too, it could go twice as fast—"

"No. Now let's go. I want this done and us out of here ASAP." He was worried about the amount of time they'd been gone. Every second increased their chances of being caught. But there was no way he was going to let Amelia out of his sight. He'd never forgive himself if anything happened to her.

They finished that boat and four others, and Cole was anticipating another moment of sweet torture as he watched Amelia's very fine bottom climbing ahead of him into the sixth boat, when the unmistakable sound of a heavy metal door opening echoed through the warehouse.

"Damn it," he swore. "Get back."

There was no place to hide. As soon as whoever had just come in turned on the lights, they were dead.

Cole grabbed Amelia and pulled her to the wall behind the boat. A few feet down was a portable scaffold with a couple of fifty-five-gallon drums on the floor next to it. A canvas drop cloth was tossed carelessly over the drums.

Cole lifted the tarp and pushed Amelia underneath just as the lights flared on. He slid in next to her.

"Give me the glow light," he whispered. He stuffed it down inside his boot and pulled his pant leg over it.

Then he wrapped his arms around her.

The sound of heavy footsteps approached.

Cole felt tension and fear radiating from Amelia's body. Each rapid beat of her pulse reverberated through him.

Even as the echoing footfalls grew closer, Cole's body reacted to the fresh strawberry scent of her hair and the supple warmth of her flesh.

If he died right here because he needed one more lungful of her sweet scent, it would be far better than the best death he'd hoped for before he'd met her. That price he would pay gladly.

The unacceptable cost was Amelia's life. So he mentally shook his head and psyched himself up to fight to the death to save her.

The guards' voices grew louder as they approached. Most of their conversation was about how much they hated working at night, and how long it would be until they could get back to their families.

The footfalls stopped right in front of their boat.

"Don't move," Cole breathed into Amelia's ear. She stiffened even more.

"Hey, what's that?" The speaker's voice rose.

Amelia gasped quietly. Cole tightened his arms around her.

"What?"

"I thought I heard something."

"Yeah?"

"Yeah, over there. Behind that boat."

For a few seconds neither guard spoke. They were listening for a rustle or a whisper. To Cole, his breaths sounded abnormally loud, as did Amelia's. But he hoped that was just his paranoia.

Still, he gauged how hard it would be for him to reach his gun, which was stuck inside his right boot. His right side was pressed against Amelia, so getting to the gun would be slow and awkward.

"I didn't hear anything," the second guard said.

"Yeah, well, trust me. I knew your hearing was going."

"There's nothing wrong with my damn hearing. I'm telling you, I didn't hear anything. Maybe you heard a rat." Cole saw the flashlight's beam through the heavy canvas that covered them.

"All right. Let's go. But keep an ear open."

"Come on, let's go."

Their footfalls faded, and a couple of seconds later the lights switched off.

When the metal exit door clanged open, Amelia wriggled. A clatter of metal against concrete sounded like a gunshot in the silence.

"Hold it," the first guard shouted. "I damn sure heard that!"

Cole heard the unmistakable sound of a weapon

being cocked. He didn't stop to think about what the wisest move was. He grabbed Amelia's hand and pulled her out from under the drop cloth.

"Run for the door," he commanded quietly, pushing her in that direction. He slid his SIG from his boot and turned toward the direction the guard had gone, keeping himself between them and Amelia.

The main door crashed shut. The guards' heavy footfalls echoed through the warehouse.

Amelia reached the emergency exit. Cole felt behind him for the door's panic bar. He pushed it.

"Run!" he commanded.

"Oh, Cole, I'm so sorry—"

"Run! Now! To the path and up. Stay low."

"What about—"

"Damn it, run!" With any luck, the guards wouldn't know about the emergency exit. They'd search the warehouse and then turn back to the main entrance. With more luck, they wouldn't sound an alarm until they'd checked out what they'd heard.

He just wanted enough time for Amelia to get back to her room safely. He hoped he could make it back, too, but she was his priority.

Amelia didn't think her legs would work. Her whole body felt limp with fear. She'd have sworn her heart had ripped in two the instant her wire cutters had hit the floor. They'd slipped from her pocket.

Her carelessness may have cost them their lives.

She lowered her head and forced one foot in front of the other until at last, she was running. She pumped her arms and legs, pushing herself as hard as she could, trying not to anticipate the feel of a bullet slamming into her back. Trying not to worry about Cole.

She heard gravel crunching and flying behind her. *Dear heavens, let it be Cole.*

"Hey! Over there!"

The shout came from way behind her, nearly drowned out by the pounding of her boots and the matching thuds of her heart.

A shot rang out. She heard it ricochet somewhere close to her.

"This way!"

More shots. More shouts.

Finally she reached the cliff path. Her breaths came in short, tight bursts. Her chest hurt. Her head was spinning with terror—for herself and for Cole.

Where was he? She didn't dare turn around and look. She was too afraid of what she'd see.

Her thighs quivered as she climbed up the cliff path until it wound around, hiding her from view of the boatyard.

She glanced around desperately. Was she hidden from view? She bent over, resting her palms on her knees and gulping lungfuls of air.

When her ears quit ringing with the sound of her own heart, she heard more shouting from below.

She wiped her face. Her hands came away greasy and mottled. And panic erupted from her very core. Camouflage face paint. Black clothes, suitable for covert operations.

What was she doing here? Running from terrorists. Running *with* a terrorist? Her greasepaint-coated hands began to tremble.

Heavy thuds surprised her.

They'd caught her. She stiffened, expecting the worst.

A figure dressed in black rounded the path.

Cole!

Without stopping, he hooked an arm around her waist and swept her with him up the path. She didn't—couldn't—speak. She let him pull her along with him, praying that they could make it back to the cliff house without being caught.

After that, she had no idea what would happen. She just ran as if the hounds of hell were after her.

As soon as Amelia pushed open the trapdoor in her closet, Cole could hear the pounding at the doors to her suite.

"Get in bed. Pull the covers up over your head."

"But—"

"Do it," he snapped.

He vaulted up through the trap door as soon as she was out of the way.

"Okay, okay!" he shouted in a growly voice he hoped sounded sleepy. "Give me a minute."

He stepped over to the suite doors. "What the hell's going on out there? This better be good." He pulled his black shirt off over his head and scrubbed at the camo greasepaint on his face.

"Chien Fou wants all hands on deck. Someone's been sneaking around in the boat warehouse."

"Aw, hell!" Cole yelled through the doors. "Who was it? Did they catch him?"

"Don't know. Open up."

"I'll be right out. Let me take a leak and get some clothes on."

"Make it quick. Leader doesn't want to lose a minute."

Cole listened until he was sure the man had left. Then he tossed his pullover in the direction of his suitcase and dropped his pants and kicked them in that direction.

Amelia sat up in bed and watched him, wide-eyed, as he headed toward the bathroom.

"Get up and clean up," he said. "And don't forget your stage makeup. Can you do something with these clothes so no one finds the greasepaint on them?"

She nodded. "I'll wash them myself. What...what's going to happen now?"

He turned on the hot-water tap in the lavatory, lathered his hands and washed the paint off his face and neck. When he was done he turned and found her standing in the bathroom doorway. "Did I get everything?"

Her eyes slid across his face, feeling like delicate fingers on his skin. "Y-yes."

Her honey-brown eyes staring out from that smeared, painted face were wide with panic. She was about two seconds away from a breakdown.

"Hang in there, Amelia. You're doing great. Get cleaned up in case Chien Fou sends for you. And don't forget, if anything happens—if they figure out it was me—I forced you."

Her throat moved as she swallowed. "I don't—"

"You *must!*" He brushed his palms across her shoulders. "I've got to go. Don't look so worried. You're safe. I promise."

"I know," she responded. "I know I'm safe with you. But the question is, are *you* safe?"

He touched her nose. "I sure as hell hope so."

IT WAS AFTER four o'clock in the morning before Cole got back to the suite. Amelia was nothing but a small lump in the bed. A few strands of hair peeked out from the covers.

Knowing she'd gone to sleep while waiting for him made his throat ache. He didn't deserve that kind of trust.

She'd left the light in the bathroom on. He saw her shirt and his hanging over the shower door, dripping onto a towel.

He turned off the light and slipped off his Windbreaker and shoes. He sat down gingerly on the edge of Amelia's bed and wearily rubbed his face with both hands.

It would be dawn soon. And before the day was over, the seven boats containing C-4 would be on their way to a rendezvous with destruction.

With a sigh he couldn't quite suppress, Cole stretched out and let his head sink back into the pillow.

Next to him, Amelia stirred. He held his breath. He didn't want to wake her. She needed as much rest as she could get.

She turned over and he saw the gleam of her sleepy eyes.

"Are you okay?" she asked.

He massaged his temples and nodded. "Go back to sleep. You have a few hours yet."

Amelia watched Cole in the dim light that filtered

in from the balcony. His face was planed in shadows that emphasized his weariness and worry. Her fingers itched to touch and soothe each line.

"I slept a little," she said. "What happened out there?"

The shadows flickered as he clenched his jaw. "The guards were sure that someone tried to break into the warehouse." He turned his head and met her gaze. "The emergency exit door was locked."

She sent him a tiny smile. "If the door is opened and the code is not entered within fifteen seconds, it locks down automatically."

"You could have saved me a few gray hairs if you'd told me that. I thought they'd find it unlocked."

"Sorry, I sort of ran out of time, and I was a little pre-occupied with other matters. Did they inspect the boats?"

He shook his head. "Since the emergency exit was locked, they decided the intruders couldn't get inside. But they searched the entire complex, including the path. They're convinced someone was sneaking around out there."

"What's going to happen now?"

"The attack's going on as planned. We leave after dark tonight."

"Tonight?" She sat up, her pulse pounding. "What about the last two boats? What are we going to do?"

"You're not going to do anything. It'll be all right."

Amelia heard the faint tinge of doubt in his voice.

"You're not sure."

"Disabling the detonators was a precaution. There's a plan in place to stop the boats."

"What plan?"

Cole leaned up on one elbow. "Can't tell you."

Amelia stared down at him.

He shook his head. "Knowing too much will put you in danger, and I'm not willing to take that chance."

"That's not a very good argument. I'm already in danger. What difference will it make if I know what the plan is?"

He sat up and pushed back against the headboard. "If Chien Fou gets the idea that you know something, he'll have you questioned. You're not trained. He'll know if you're lying. And he's got very creative methods for forcing people to talk." Cole's face turned dark as he talked. He shook his head, his gray eyes heated.

Creative methods. Amelia shuddered. "I suppose I should thank you for protecting me."

"Just doing my job, ma'am," he said, obviously trying to lighten her mood.

"I'm serious." She studied him, acknowledging the truth that she still had no idea whether he was a good guy or a bad guy. A terrorist, or an honorable, patriotic undercover agent. She knew what her heart believed. But hearts were notorious for not listening to reason.

The truth lies in a kiss. Where had that come from? She met his gaze. Leaning toward him, she looked at his mouth, at his strong jaw, his beautifully chiseled features, his gray eyes—too clear to hide deceit.

"So very serious," she repeated. "Thank you for protecting me and my father. Thank you for…" Her voice died as her eyes came back to his lips.

Before her brain even acknowledged what was about to happen, Amelia leaned over and pressed a kiss to his cheek.

He hadn't shaved and his stubble tickled and pricked her lips. Her head filled with his bittersweet chocolate scent.

He turned his head slightly, just enough that his lips touched hers. It could have been an accident. He could have meant to pull away and accidentally brushed against her lips in passing.

But he didn't pull away. His mouth lingered there, barely touching hers, holding her paralyzed just by the connection of her mouth to his.

His hand came up and encircled her neck and she was lost. She let him pull her closer—closer, until somehow she was straddling his lap and his erection was pressing against the faint barrier of her panties.

"Cole—" she gasped.

His hands bunched the satiny material of her sleep shirt. He pushed it out of the way and his warm palms and fingers caressed her bare waist. His mouth still held her.

The way his tongue moved and tasted and delved was driving her crazy with need.

She wrapped her fingers around his neck and gave him back kiss for kiss. Truth for truth.

If the voice in her head was right and the truth lay in a kiss, then she was opening her whole life, her whole being, to the truth of her feelings for the mysterious stranger who'd brought danger and terror with him into her life.

"Amelia—" Cole gasped.

"No." She pressed her fingers against his mouth, then replaced them with her lips. "Don't say anything." Her lips moved against his. "I don't know what's going to happen, but I know one thing for sure. I have to know who you are, Cole Robinson, and there's only one way I know of to do it."

His hand cupped the back of her head and he kissed her more deeply, more thoroughly than he had so far. So deeply that he stole what little willpower she had left—sucked it right out of her with her breath.

His erection pulsed against her, drawing tiny answering pulses from her. She pushed against him, rubbed against him, until she thought she was going to explode.

His hands slid back to her waist and then lower, until his thumbs were rubbing in little circles just at the edge of her center.

Cole teased Amelia, pushing closer and closer to her hot, liquid center, but not coming close enough to tip her over the edge.

She straightened and arched her neck. Her breasts puckered against the delicate satiny sleep shirt she wore. He wrapped one arm around her waist and pulled himself upright so he could reach her mouth.

She moaned, deep in her throat, and kissed him. Her other hand touched him through the material of his jeans, sending an electric shock all the way out to his fingers and toes.

"Ah, Amelia, don't."

But she didn't listen. She pressed against him in a rhythm so exquisitely torturous that he knew he was going to explode in just a few seconds.

"Stop," he begged, pushing her hand away. "Let me get rid of these clothes." He sat up and leaned over, kissing her while he unbuttoned his jeans.

Within seconds his clothes were gone and he'd slid her shirt off over her head.

He knew what he wanted now. He wanted her—all of her. He craved the feel of her body pressed against his. He stretched out and pulled her close. Her skin was hot and deliciously supple. He kissed and nipped at her breasts until their tips were rigid. Then he bent lower and spread her legs gently apart.

A tiny gasp escaped her lips and she slid her fingers into his hair. When he touched her and then tasted her, her fingers tightened into a fist.

Her back arched, giving him more access. She tasted like a woman, dark and fresh, and totally sexual.

"Cole, please," she panted, tugging on his hair.

He ignored her for a few more seconds, driving himself wild as he brought her closer and closer to ecstasy.

Finally he gave in and kissed his way up her body to her mouth. This time when he kissed her, he spread himself over her, giving her a full-body kiss.

Her fingers wrapped around him. "Cole?"

Doing his best to hold on to his sanity, he lifted himself up and entered her, shuddering with reaction.

Amelia gasped at the sensation of Cole filling her. She'd never felt as filled with sensation, as complete, as she did joined with Cole. Their bodies fit, molded together like two halves of a whole.

Then he began to move, and Amelia could do nothing but move with him, meeting each thrust with her answering rhythm, until the room began to swirl and the smell of roses and Cole filled her senses. She lost all sense of herself. It was only them, together, acting and feeling as one.

Then she flared like a supernova.

Chapter Twelve

Danger.

Cole opened his eyes. Before his brain even considered why he'd been startled awake, another thought formed and he'd whirled and vaulted out of bed.

Several things hit his brain at once. He was naked. The clock on Amelia's bedside table read 8:00 a.m. He and she had made love. And something bad was happening.

Amelia turned over and sat up. Cole put his finger against his lips. "Get dressed," he mouthed. "Now!"

He grabbed his jeans and tugged his discarded shirt over his head, then stuck his feet in his boots and quickly laced them. Then he reached for his gun, which he'd laid on the table beside the bed.

By the time he straightened, Amelia had her black jeans on and was reaching for a sweater.

"What's going on?" she whispered as she tied her climbing boots.

"I don't know. I heard something." He motioned her around the bed. "Get into the bathroom. Remember, if anything happens, I forced you."

"I am not going to—"

A commotion rose just outside the door to the suite. Cole pushed Amelia toward the bathroom while keeping his attention on the double doors.

With a deafening crash, the doors flew open. Two seconds later, he heard a noise from the trapdoor in Amelia's closet swing open.

They were caught.

Cole cursed himself for a fool. He should have pulled that damn rope ladder in behind him—the hauling rope, too.

Too late now. Chien Fou had made him. He was a dead man.

Searing regret burned through his heart. He ignored it. There'd be time for that later, while he waited to see how Chien Fou would kill him.

Right now, he had to save Amelia. So he grabbed her and pulled her around in front of him. He caught her in a chokehold and held his gun to her temple.

"I forced you. I beat you. I'm the bad guy," he whispered in her ear.

"No, Cole—"

He stopped her protest by cutting off her breath for a brief instant. If the guards heard her and found out she'd helped him, they'd kill her—or worse. He'd die before he'd let that happen.

He was going down alone.

"Cole, let her go and get your hands up," Abel ordered. "Chien Fou wants to talk to you."

"No way!" he shouted. "Not till I find out what's going on. Why did you break in?" He sounded as if he was on the verge of hysteria. Not a huge stretch. And it served his purposes. He wanted them to think he was out of control. Crazy enough to kill Amelia if they rushed him.

He heard the closet door open. A man emerged from the trapdoor. It was one of Chien Fou's personal bodyguards.

Cole twisted. "What the hell? Where'd you come from?"

"Please, Cole," he said. "Don't insult my intelligence. We know you've been sneaking in and out. We saw the footprints."

"I don't know what you're talking about," he snapped, hoping to buy some time. He had no idea what he was going to do, but he knew he had to make it appear as if Amelia was just a pawn in his game.

A shot rang out. Cole felt something slam into his left shoulder. It spun him sideways and he lost his grip on Amelia.

He staggered, just as the unmistakable chill of a gun barrel pressed into the side of his neck.

"Drop the gun."

Cole did it. The sensation of pain was creeping into his brain. Pain and sticky warmth. From his shoulder. He'd been shot.

Amelia cried out. He whirled—too fast. His vision went black for an instant. Then he saw her. Abel had his hands on her. At the same time, a guard jerked his arms behind his back and cuffed him. He gasped at the pain in his shoulder.

"Move," Abel snarled.

They were taking them to Chien Fou. He prayed that, even if the Global Freedom Front leader ordered him killed, he'd think Amelia was worth more alive— and—as Cole had pointed out to him earlier—undamaged.

With Chien Fou's bodyguard leading the way, he and Amelia were marched up the stairs to Chien Fou's suite.

Chien Fou was in his customary place—still with two guards flanking him. A third man stood behind them, near the window. Cole had never seen the third man before, but he recognized the second man. It was the electrician. The man who'd turned cell phones, wires and blasting caps into lethal weapons.

The presence of the electrician meant only one thing. They'd discovered the disarmed detonators.

He'd failed. Like an ice cube in hot water, the last of Cole's hope dissolved.

Chien Fou's bodyguard stepped over and took the electrician's place beside his leader.

"Cole, my friend," Chien Fou said. "I'm so disappointed. I thought we'd become close."

In your dreams. "What the hell's going on, *Leader?* Your idiot guard *shot* me!"

"Silence!" Chien Fou waved a hand. "From this point on, you will speak only when spoken to. What is it, Cole? Money? Were you *paid* to infiltrate us for three years?"

Chien Fou's black eyes narrowed. "No. I've been thinking about this ever since I found out you'd sneaked out of the house. You are not in this for the money. You're doing it for your country, aren't you?"

Cole smiled. "Don't be ridiculous."

Chien Fou's gaze flickered and he nodded at the guard next to Cole.

The man rammed the butt of his gun into Cole's shoulder.

The pain bent him double. Nausea engulfed him. From somewhere outside the orb of agony, he heard a distressed cry.

Don't, he pleaded silently. If Amelia reacted to what they were doing to him, Chien Fou would know she wasn't Cole's hostage.

"Look at me, Cole."

The guard who'd rammed him pushed the barrel of his gun into Cole's neck and forced his head up. He straightened as much as he could, swaying and gulping huge lungfuls of air as the pain and nausea ratcheted up.

"I want to know how much the government knows about our plan, and what their counterattack is."

Sweat formed on Cole's brow and tickled his cheek and neck. He tried to swallow but his mouth was too dry. The pain surrounded him—he was choking on it, drowning in it. From a reserve of strength he hadn't known existed, he dredged up a response. "I don't—" his voice croaked "—know what you're talking about."

The gun barrel sank into his neck and forced his head back. Blood roared in his ears and stars exploded behind his eyelids. His vision went black. He stumbled, then sank to his knees.

"Look at me!" Chien Fou yelled.

Someone grabbed his hair and jerked his head up. Cole opened his eyes.

Chien Fou was sipping water, his black eyes glittering over the top of the glass. "Miss Hopkins seems more concerned about you than frightened of you. That disappoints me greatly. You told me you were taking care of her." He gestured with his head.

Cole stiffened involuntarily. A millisecond later pain exploded in his middle back. He fell forward as his muscles cramped. Twisting, he tried to ignore the searing pain in his shoulder and get his knees under him. But with his hands cuffed behind his back and his muscles cramping with tension, he floundered.

The guard grabbed a handful of his shirt and pulled him up to his knees.

Cole tried to shake off the haze of pain. "She just prefers my hands on her to yours," he growled through clenched teeth, desperate to try to save her.

"Your chivalry is admirable, Cole. But sadly, now that we have the C-4 in place and the boats are ready to go, I have no further use for her."

Amelia heard Chien Fou's words, but they barely registered. She couldn't take her eyes off Cole. She was afraid if she looked away from him for even one second, he'd falter and die. As long as she could use her will to keep him alive, she would.

But he'd lost too much blood. Enough to turn his white T-shirt dark. He'd endured crushing blows to his belly and kidneys and to his wounded shoulder.

Plus, from the way he was wavering, it was obvious he was barely conscious.

"Miss Hopkins."

She let her eyes flicker toward Chien Fou.

"I'd like to introduce you to Dr. Singh. He has already sedated your father and the mayor."

Amelia started. "My father?"

"Yes. They're locked inside one of the boats—"

"I want to see him."

Chien Fou's mouth drew down into a frown. The guard standing beside her straightened, but apparently the leader decided not to punish her for interrupting him. "You won't see him again in this life. Dr. Singh will sedate you in just a few minutes. You will be placed in one of the boats. Dr. Singh assures me the dose of the sedative is enough to keep you unconscious through the explosions." He smiled. "Too bad you won't get to see the display. It should be quite fantastic."

Amelia's head spun with the horror of Chien Fou's plan. He was putting them aboard the floating bombs. They would die when the boats exploded.

"You'll never get away with this," she snapped.

"Of course I will." Chien Fou gestured. The guard standing beside her wrenched her arms behind her back and cuffed her.

"Guard, please take a bottle of water and revive Cole."

The guard took the water and poured it over Cole's head. He jerked and straightened. His face was pale and blood was still spreading across the front and back of his T-shirt.

"Cole, I need some answers. My men found the cut wires, and Oren, my electrician, has replaced them. I have a man searching your things now. I fully expect to find electronic equipment there. Possibly a telephone that transmits via satellite?"

Cole stared at him without changing his facial expression.

Amelia saw Chien Fou's fingers twitch, and she bit her lip to keep from crying out a warning.

The guard next to Cole backhanded him across the

mouth. He fell backward. The guard jerked him back to his knees.

Something inside Cole, something besides physical strength, kept him upright. Amelia knew she was watching true courage.

"Let's try this again, Cole. Have you been communicating with someone via a satellite phone?"

Behind Amelia, a knock sounded on the door and she heard it open.

"Ah, here's my answer now. What did you find?"

The man who handed the tiny phone to Chien Fou was young—maybe not even twenty-five. What made these very different people come together for the purpose of destroying America?

"So Cole, it *is* a satellite phone. And if I were to press redial, who would I find on the other end?"

Cole remained stoic. He kept his gaze on Chien Fou's face.

"Right," Chien Fou said, and tossed the phone back to the young man. "Hold on to that, but do not activate it. I have a feeling whoever is on the other end is expecting a particular response. If he hears anything else, who knows what he might do?"

Chien Fou turned back to Cole. "My guess is that you have informed your contact about everything that has happened thus far. And he's now waiting to hear from you about the specifics. When we will be leaving. Our specific destinations, and so on. Since I have not told any of my men the specific targets, there's no way you can know them." He nodded at Cole's guard. "Pick him up. Set him on his feet, if he doesn't topple over."

Once Cole was standing, Chien Fou motioned for

him to be brought closer. "I don't suppose I can per-suade you to make that call and feed your contact false information for me?"

Amelia saw Cole's struggle not to falter. Blood dripped down his arm. His face had turned from merely pale to a sickly green. His eyes were glazed with pain. Still, he lifted his chin and managed to shake his head.

"I'd...die first."

Chien Fou sighed. "I was afraid of that. Too bad. I'm certain you had an arranged contact time. Therefore your contact will know you've been compromised. And that means they will either come storming down here to rescue you, or they'll mount defenses on every major target on the Eastern Seaboard. But without your specific informa-tion, it will be difficult for them to adequately defend every seaport. And, since I'm planning to attack smaller yet still vital ports, they will likely miss us completely."

"You won't succeed," Cole muttered.

"Dr. Singh. Please, administer the sedative. We need to be on our way soon after dark." He looked at Cole and then at Amelia.

"One of my biggest regrets is that I do not have the manpower to guard you until all the boats get to the targets. If I did, I'd leave you awake for the big event. So you could experience the explosions first-hand."

THE FIRST THING Cole was aware of was surprise that he was still alive. He knew he was because of the pain. His left shoulder felt as if someone had dug a hole in it and set fire to it. The smell of blood burned his nostrils. Nausea ripped at his guts and bats were beating their wings against the inside of his head.

He wanted to sink back into oblivion, but for some reason that sounded like a bad idea. There was something he needed to do. Something he needed to stay alive for.

First and foremost, he needed to figure out where he was. He was lying on something, and besides the pain and nausea, other discomforts were coming to light. His hands were in a weird position behind him. He flexed his fingers—or tried to. They were numb.

His nose was buried in a corner—an upholstered corner. The material was scratchy and smelled of dye and the ocean.

Ocean.

Danger.

He tried to sit up, but moving did all sorts of nasty things to his head and stomach. A groan escaped his dry lips.

He finally forced his eyes open. Then, with a huge effort, he turned over. The movement caused his stomach to clench and he retched dryly and coughed.

Something was horribly wrong. He should know what it was, but so far, he hadn't been able to make his hazy brain hang on to one thought long enough to make sense of it.

He squinted and peered around him. Damn it, even his eyeballs hurt.

Concentrate, he commanded himself. He still smelled blood. Straining his neck, he looked down at himself.

So there it was.

Blood.

Lots of it. Too much. And he had the sickening feeling it was all his.

A memory pushed its way past the pain and gut-wrenching nausea.

Amelia. Where was Amelia?

He squinted, struggling to orient himself. The room looked familiar and smelled of new upholstery and the sea.

Then it dawned on him. He was on a settee in the master stateroom of one of the yachts. He saw a small lump on the king-size bed.

Amelia. He pushed himself up and bent double as his belly cramped and he heaved again.

With the surge of nausea, all his memories came flooding back.

They were on a boat—a moving boat. Chien Fou had cuffed their hands behind their backs and sedated them.

He'd planted them inside one of his floating bombs. Cole didn't know how much time they had, but he knew it wasn't much. If he could trust his senses, it was just after dawn and the boat was moving along at a steady clip.

Now that he could think, he recognized the soft whirr of the autopilot. Its sound triggered more memories. Each of the boats was guided by electromagnetic sensors and programmed to travel straight for its target, the massive steel hull of an oil supertanker.

They probably had less than an hour before Chien Fou detonated the C-4 loaded in each yacht.

Alarm cleared the haze from his brain. He had work to do. Sharp pain in his wrists reminded him that he was helpless with his hands cuffed behind his back.

He looked over at Amelia, lying unconscious on the bed. "Amelia," he called.

She didn't move.

"Amelia. Come on. Wake up." He pushed himself to his feet, gritting his teeth against dizziness and nausea, then tumbled onto the bed, beside her.

After a few seconds of searing pain, he forced himself to inch toward her. He nudged her shoulder with his nose.

"Amelia!"

She moaned.

"Come on, Amelia, wake up. I need your help."

"Cole?" she muttered sleepily.

"Amelia, listen to me. You've been sedated. You've got to fight it."

"Fight it," she murmured. "Got to—" But she didn't move. After a couple of seconds, her breaths evened out again.

"Come on, Amelia." He nudged her again.

"No…" she whined sleepily.

What could he do to wake her up? He couldn't grab her or shake her. Not with his hands cuffed behind his back.

So he leaned over and kissed her, and when he did, erotic memories flooded his hazy brain. Memories of making love with her, of holding her, kissing her, feeling her warmth enveloping him. He remembered how she looked at him as she came.

He didn't remember how it had happened. Or why he hadn't had sense enough to stop it.

But he would never forget the feel of her, the smell, the taste, the sensation of her. And remembering, even through the drowsiness and pain, and despite the urgency of their situation, he grew hard.

He nosed a strand of hair away from her face and

pressed kisses against her cheek, her temple, her eyelids. To wake her, he reminded himself.

"Amelia, wake up for me. We don't have much of a chance, but I've got no chance at all without you."

She murmured something.

"Good. Come on, Amelia." He kissed her mouth and nibbled at her lower lip. "Come on."

"Cole?" she whispered. At least that's what he thought she said.

"Yeah, sweetie. It's me. Cole." He blew on her eyelids.

She squeezed them tight, then opened them to narrow slits.

"Amelia!" He pushed a commanding tone into his voice. "Amelia, wake up—now!"

Her eyes flew open. "Cole? Wha—"

"Wake up. Stay with me."

"Where…? What?" She blinked and cast her bleary gaze around the stateroom. "Where are we?"

"We're on one of the boats. I need your help. I can't do this without you."

She frowned at him, and he saw her consciousness slipping.

"Amelia!"

She straightened and promptly rolled over onto her side. "Ow. Dear heavens, I'm handcuffed." She struggled to sit up.

"Me, too. Listen, I'm not moving too well. Can you manage to get to the toolbox? We need the wire cutters."

She was getting that glazed look in her eye again.

"Stay with me, Amelia."

She shook her head. "How can you stay awake?"

"I don't know. The pain?" he said wryly. "Can you stand up?"

She shook her head. "No. Can't we just sleep?"

He sat up as straight as he could. "Amelia, listen to me. It's after dawn. Within an hour, Chien Fou is going to transmit the signal that will blow up this boat and all the others, including your father's."

Amelia's eyes widened and Cole felt an acute triumph. He'd gotten through to her.

"My dad. The oil tankers." All the drowsiness left her face and she sat up. "What can we do? Oh—my shoulders hurt so bad."

"See if you can get to the toolbox and grasp a pair of wire cutters in your hand. If you can, then bring them to me."

She blinked. "Oh, Cole. You're covered with blood." Horror darkened her eyes. "You've been shot. I've got to stop the bleeding."

"Amelia, we've got bigger problems."

"Wait a minute, Cole." She rolled over onto her side. "What are you—?"

"I know what I can do." She kicked off her shoes, then began wriggling and grunting. She sat on her cuffed hands and began working them down her legs.

He watched her, openmouthed. When he finally figured out what she was doing, admiration and amusement commingled inside him, blotting out the pain for a few seconds. "Can you really do that?"

Even as the words left his mouth, he saw that she *was* doing it. She bent her knees and kept working. She tugged and grunted until the cuffs finally slipped under her heels. "Ow, this was a lot easier in my yoga class."

"What the hell—?"

"One week our instructor had us clasp our hands in back and then work them around to the front without letting go." She grimaced. "It was…a lot easier than…this," she muttered,

If she could actually get her hands in front, they'd have a chance. She might be able to save them.

Finally, she'd done it. Her cuffed hands were in front of her. Her wrists were rubbed raw. Perspiration dripped from her forehead, and she was breathing heavily, but her eyes glimmered with success.

"You did it," he said. "Are your wrists okay? Is that blood?"

She looked at her wrists, then at his shirt. "I've lost a drop. You look like you've lost at least a quart."

"Can you get the wire cutters and snip those wires on the detonator first? Chien Fou could activate the blasting caps any second."

Amelia slid off the bed and hurried up into the pilothouse. Although moving around was *much* easier with her hands cuffed in front instead of in back, it still wasn't easy. She dug in the toolbox until her fingers closed around a pair of wire cutters.

She turned around and ran below again. By the time she got back to the stateroom, Cole had maneuvered to the edge of the bed. She could see in his face and body what the effort had cost him. His face had a greenish cast. He was shivering, and his eyes were glazing over. When she'd said he looked like he'd lost a quart of blood, she hadn't been exaggerating. She was afraid he was in shock.

"Cut the wires," he muttered without looking up. "Hurry."

Behind the settee, sitting on top of the gray blob of C-4, sat the gadget Chien Fou's electrician had hooked up. A cell phone was connected by wires to the detonator, which in turn was attached to a blasting cap.

She remembered which wires Cole had cut in the other boat, so she repeated the process, quickly and efficiently disabling the detonator.

There. Thank heavens. At least now the boat wouldn't blow up under them. For a couple of seconds her eyes drifted shut. She was so tired, and sleep sounded really good.

"Amelia?" Cole's voice drew her out of her drug-induced haze. She had a job to do. She stared at the mess of wires and metal and plastic—*the cell phone.*

Her heart jumped. Adrenaline surged through her blood. She grabbed up the whole mess and ran into the stateroom.

Cole was slumped against the settee back.

"Cole? Wake up, please."

He stirred without opening his eyes.

"Please, Cole. Wake up. Listen to me, please. Look what I have."

He blinked and his head lolled.

"Look, Cole." She put her fingers under his chin and lifted his head. "Wake up, please."

He opened his eyes and tried to meet her gaze.

He was hurt so badly. *Dear God, please don't let him die. I love him.*

"Look, Cole. It's a cell phone," she said. "Cole, it's the cell phone that was hooked up to the explosive."

"Can't think." His head drooped to his chest.

"Yes, you can. Listen to me, Cole. Just a couple

more minutes. We're going to beat them. All you have to do is direct me."

"D-rect—"

Amelia wanted to cry. She was losing him. Somehow she knew if he lost consciousness right now, she'd lose him forever.

"Cole. There are all these wires. What do I do with them? Help me."

He didn't move for an agonizingly long few seconds. Finally he opened his eyes and peered at the mess of wires. "Got to disconnect…the wires."

With Cole guiding her, Amelia managed to separate the wires from the ringer on the cell phone.

"It turned off. Cole. The phone turned off."

He rubbed his eyes. "Wiggle the battery. Might be loose."

She pushed on the battery and to her delight, the phone display lit up. She pressed the button to reveal incoming calls.

"Cole, all the calls are from the same number."

"Right." Cole retched and coughed. His whole body was shivering. "Makes sense. Chien Fou's phone."

Amelia stared at him. "How do you—"

"Testing. He was testing the c-connection."

"So all the boats have phones programmed to the same number?"

"Only way. All boats…go up at the s-same time."

Cole lifted his head. His face was dripping sweat. His teeth were chattering, but his eyes were clear—at least for now. "We can stop him." He took a shaky breath. "Dial this number and hold…hold phone to my ear."

He recited the number.

When Amelia heard the ring, she held the phone to his ear.

"Patrick," he said. "I've got the…" He paused, listening. "Mission is…priority."

The same words he'd used when she'd overheard him on her balcony. Some kind of code, she figured.

His head drooped. "Tell him," he whispered. "Amelia—"

She raised the phone to her ear. "Cole's been shot," she told the anonymous person on the other end. "I've got the cell number that Chien Fou is going to use to detonate the explosive."

"Give it to me," a deep voice commanded.

She recited the number. She heard the man speak to someone.

"We're about to block the signal. Where are you?"

"On one of the boats."

She heard a muttered curse. "Do you know where?"

"No. We were drugged." She noticed a change in the noise of the engine. "Dear heavens, the boat just sped up."

"What's going on?"

She pushed herself up off the bed and ran into the main salon and up the stairs to the pilothouse. The sight that greeted her nearly paralyzed her with shock. The dark steel hull of a supertanker was directly in front of them.

The autopilot. It was still engaged. They were speeding toward the port side of the ship's bow.

"We're headed for the supertanker! All the boats are going to crash into the ships. You've got to stop them—"

"How long?"

Amelia's heart was racing so hard she could barely breathe, much less think, but the expertise and understanding of motor yachts that her father had taught her all her life kicked in. She measured the distance with her eyes.

"Maximum speed is thirty knots. We're aimed at the tip of the port side of the nose. Seven minutes max. Have the tankers veer to port—hard! We just might miss the tip."

"Send up a flare."

"I have to try to steer the boat to port—to miss the tanker!"

"Fire the flare first! We're alerting the tankers and blocking the phone signal now."

The phone went dead. She dropped it and dove for the toolbox, grabbing the flare gun and stuffing a flare into it.

She opened the pilothouse door and fired it straight up. Then she loaded and fired a second flare and a third.

Praying that shooting the flares hadn't taken too long, she grabbed the wheel with both hands and wrenched it to port as hard as she could. The boat veered alarmingly, nearly keeling over. She tried to back off the power but the autopilot overrode her. So she hung on to the wheel for dear life as she watched the supertanker grow closer and closer. Finally, the boat's bow veered toward open water. She let the wheel slide through her fingers and straightened the boat.

She'd turned enough to miss the tanker they were aimed for, but what about the other boats?

What about her father?

Her hands were shaking and she felt woozy. All she wanted to do was collapse. But she had to check on Cole.

She forced her legs to carry her below, to the master stateroom.

Cole hadn't moved. His head lolled on his chest and his shoulders were slumped. His chest rose and fell with fast, shallow breaths.

"They blocked the signal," she whispered shakily, awed by the magnitude of what had just happened. "You stopped Chien Fou."

Cole's breath escaped in a sigh of relief. "No," he croaked. "You did."

"The other boats are heading for the tankers. I don't know if the tankers can steer enough to avoid them."

He didn't say anything.

She touched his face and was horrified at how cold and clammy his skin was.

"Cole? I've got to do something. You're still bleeding. I've got to stop it." Amelia grabbed a corner of the bedspread and pressed it against Cole's shoulder, even though she knew it was probably too late. When she pressed on his wound, more blood came out.

"Oh, no," she whispered. "No, no, no. Don't die, Cole. I'll kill you if you die now."

Cole couldn't speak, couldn't move. He'd lost too much blood, he knew. The weakness he felt was pathological—fatal.

Amelia's hands pressing on his shoulder hurt like hell. He wanted to tell her to stop wasting her energy on a dead man, but he didn't want to suck away the last of her hope. If he had to die, this was how he'd prefer to do it. With her by his side.

Suddenly he felt a surge of renewed hope. For the first time since his father's betrayal, Cole actually believed he could survive it. Also for the first time, he had someone he wanted to live for. Ironic, since he was about to die.

He noticed Amelia's breaths were becoming more even, softer. "Hey," he murmured. "Are you going to sleep on me?"

"No." But her voice was low and drowsy. "I'm going to hold on, I promise. I won't let go."

"I know."

"Cole, promise me you won't leave me."

"I—" He faltered. How could he make that promise, when he felt the life seeping out of him with every beat of his heart?

Instead, he turned his head and pressed his lips against her temple. "Good night, sleeping beauty."

His last thought was how wonderful it would be to be able to say that to her every night for the rest of his life. His last prayer was that he'd have the chance.

Chapter Thirteen

Amelia awoke to the sounds of shouts and heavy boots on the deck above her head. She forced her eyelids open as the boots thudded closer.

"Here! We've got two!"

Men in dark green, carrying large guns and sporting transmitters in their ears, appeared in the doorway of the stateroom.

"Help Cole," she muttered, trying to hold her eyes open. "He's lost so much blood. And he's still bleeding." She couldn't stop pressing on his shoulder. If she did, she was afraid the last bit of his blood would spill and he'd die. There was so much of it already, on his shirt, on her hands, soaking the corner of the bedspread she was holding.

"Ma'am, you can let go now." A man tried to push her hands away.

"No," she protested. "I've got to hold on. I promised."

"I understand," the man said. "But we've got to get him into the helicopter so we can take good care of him."

She struggled, but she was no match for the man. He

pulled her away as two other men crowded into the stateroom and started unloading bags and yelling orders.

The man who had hold of her hands pulled her out through the door and handed her off to some other men, who carried her up on deck. A massive roaring filled the air and the wind whipped her hair around her face.

"We've got you, ma'am. What's your name?"

"What?" She couldn't hear above the roar of wind.

"Your name."

"Ah-mee-lee-yah," she said, pronouncing it the way Cole did.

"Okay, Amelia, we're going to fasten this strap around you and hand you over to Joe here, who's going to carry you up into the helicopter."

"The what?" She frowned, trying to make sense of what they were saying.

"Just let us do our jobs," one of the men yelled in her ear. "We're going to take good care of you."

And somehow, they did. The next thing she knew she was floating through the air, with Joe's arms around her. She kept her eyes closed tight and her head buried in Joe's stiff, scratchy collar.

Then other people grabbed her and soon she found herself lying on a stretcher. A young man leaned over her.

"You're going to feel a little prick in your arm. Don't worry about it. Before you know it, we'll be back on the ground."

"We're not on the ground?" she asked, but he didn't pay any attention to her.

She felt the little prick, and soon her head was

floating hazily above her body—or at least that's what it felt like.

She could hear people talking and yelling, but it didn't seem to be connected with her. She felt as if she had wandered onto the set of a movie, and everyone knew their lines but her.

Careful—lost a lot of blood.

—still alive?

Three units of plasma—

—what the hell happened to them?

The men had stopped hovering over her and were hovering over someone else they'd placed on a stretcher beside her.

She didn't hear Cole's voice, but she was sure he was one of them. He'd promised her he wouldn't leave her—hadn't he?

AMELIA OPENED HER EYES. Her head was pounding and she had a sharp, metallic taste in her mouth. She was lying on a stretcher. A woman was trying to place a mask over her face.

"No! Stop!" she shouted, pushing at the mask. "What are you doing?"

"Ms. Hopkins, we're about to transport you to the hospital. We need you to lie back down on the stretcher."

The roaring was still in her ears. She twisted her head and saw a military-green helicopter. Was that the source of the roaring and the wind?

"What happened? I was on a boat—where's Cole?" She sat up, ignoring the wooziness in her head, and squinted in the bright sunlight.

Nobody answered her.

"Where is Cole?" She pushed the mask away when the woman tried to place it over her face again.

The helicopter. Cole was in the helicopter. He'd promised her something.

Two soldiers climbed down out of the copter, then reached back inside for something. It was a stretcher. As they pulled the stretcher out hand over hand, two more soldiers approached and took hold of it.

Amelia blinked and held up her hand, trying to block both the wind from the helicopter blades and the sunlight.

The stretcher had someone on it. She rubbed her eyes and looked again.

Whoever was on the stretcher was covered—with a blanket.

Covered.

Her heart seized.

"No!" She pushed at the nurse's arms. "No, no, no. Let go of me."

"Ms. Hopkins. Calm down or I'll have to sedate you."

"No! Not Cole!" Amelia swung at the nurse, connecting with the woman's neck. She pushed herself up and threw herself at the door of the ambulance.

Two soldiers caught her before she hit the ground.

The four stretcher-bearers solemnly carried the covered stretcher toward a second ambulance.

"Please!" she begged. "Let me go! I need to see him. I have to—"

"Amelia," a strong, vaguely familiar voice said.

She blinked at him. "Who—?"

"I'm Patrick Hayes, with Homeland Security." His mouth curved in a wry smile. "We talked on the phone.

We found your father. He and the mayor were back at the boatyard, in a warehouse. He's at the hospital."

"He's alive? He's all right? Thank God. But where's Cole?"

Patrick Hayes's gaze faltered. "I wanted to tell you that only three of the boats hit tankers, and only minor damage was done to the tankers' hulls."

Amelia closed her eyes in an instant of relief that Chien Fou's plan was thwarted. Then she met the Homeland Security agent's gaze. "I need to see Cole."

Hayes shook his head. "I'm sorry, Amelia. I can't let you. This is how it has to be."

She tried to sit up, but Hayes put his hand on her shoulders. "Don't hurt yourself," he warned.

She couldn't take her eyes off the covered stretcher as it was carefully lifted into the ambulance and the doors were closed.

Helplessly, she watched as it drove away.

A commotion on the other side of the tarmac caught her eye. There were soldiers with MP badges on their sleeves, marching several men to an armored truck. Chien Fou and his two bodyguards were in front. Behind them were several other guards she recognized.

Chien Fou had watched the ambulance pull away, too. Then he turned his black eyes toward her. Just as he did, one of the MPs nudged him with the automatic rifle he was carrying.

Amelia closed her eyes. The leader of the Global Freedom Front had been stopped. Cole had succeeded in his mission. Tears seeped out between her eyelids.

But was the price worth it?

That was an unfair question. Even as it bloomed in

her mind, she knew it. Of course the price was worth paying. Any price was worth freedom.

But why? Why did it have to be Cole?

"He's a hero," Patrick Hayes muttered, as he nodded to the nurse and then stepped aside.

Amelia clenched her fists. Let them be proud of Cole for dying a hero. All she could do was grieve.

Two nurses lifted the stretcher up into the ambulance and a third nurse held up a syringe.

"I'm going to give you a sedative now, and when you wake up, you'll be in the hospital. Now lie down. And, Ms. Hopkins? I am so very sorry."

AMELIA STOOD AT the door of the main assembly room of the Hopkins Boatworks's office building, listening to Rick Simpson, the new mayor of Raven's Cliff, talk about the latest horror the town had gone through.

He mentioned Ross Fancher, whose death was being deemed heroic. He'd died at the hands of terrorists.

Amelia was glad that Ross's family finally had closure, but her thoughts were on the last time she'd stood in this room. She'd been standing next to Cole when he'd told Hopkins employees about the *secret government plan* to thwart a terrorist attack.

She hadn't known at the time that the words Cole was saying were true. She hadn't known then that he was a hero. Her eyes filled with tears, just as they had every single day for the past three weeks.

Cole. She'd missed him every day. She knew she would miss him every day for the rest of her life.

Her father squeezed her shoulders and pressed a kiss to her temple. "Hang in there, sweet pea."

She blinked away tears and smiled at him. "I'm fine. I understand why the new mayor wants to honor you—"

"And you. And don't forget the presidential citation."

She nodded. "I know. But for me, today is for Cole." Her voice broke.

Her dad squeezed her shoulders again. "I agree. He's a remarkable young man."

Yes, he was.

The new mayor finally changed the tone of his voice. He looked across the roomful of people at Amelia and her father, and smiled.

"Ladies and gentlemen, I'd like to present to you the latest heroes of the great town of Raven's Cliff, Amelia Hopkins and her father, Reginald Hopkins, two very brave and patriotic Americans."

The room erupted with applause and cheers.

Amelia's father held out his hand, so she preceded him up to the front of the room. As she and her dad stepped up to the dais, the mayor added his applause to everyone else's.

The townspeople rose as one in a standing ovation. Finally the mayor raised his hands.

"Okay, everyone. Let's get on with the ceremony. Then we can adjourn to the cafeteria, where a huge spread has been laid out for all of us."

He opened an official-looking folder and read the citation of bravery signed by the President of the United States, and addressed to Amelia and Reginald Hopkins.

Amelia couldn't keep tears of pride, gratitude and grief from cascading down her face as the accolades went on and on.

She smiled and held her dad's hand as the townspeople offered up another round of applause and cheers.

As she looked out over the sea of faces—most of whom she'd known all her life, her eyes lit on a face that was familiar, but for a different reason.

It was the fortune-teller from the Boat Fest. Had that just been four weeks ago? It seemed like a lifetime.

The woman's red-painted lips broadened in a smile, and Amelia remembered her words.

For you, the journey to love will be a long one, and fraught with danger.

She bit her lip. *Journey to love.* The fortune-teller had told the truth, as far as she'd gone. But she hadn't finished her prophecy.

Why didn't you tell me my journey would end in grief? she silently asked the woman.

Because then you would have missed the love.

Amelia blinked and glanced around. There was no woman near her. But the voice was definitely female. She looked back at the fortune-teller.

Had the woman's lips moved? She was sure they hadn't. So how had she heard her voice in her head? Even from across the room, she could see the sparkle in the fortune-teller's blue eyes.

Then her father took her hand. "Let's go, Amelia. We don't want to miss the lunch."

Amelia smiled indulgently. Her father had been feeling much better lately, and that was a blessing.

But he led her not toward the cafeteria, but in the opposite direction, to the door behind the dais and through the hallway to her office.

"Where are we going?"

Her father smiled. "We need to pick up something."

As they approached her office, the door opened.

"Dad, what—?"

Two men in dark suits stepped out and stood, one on each side of the door.

"It's okay. Go on in."

She stepped past the men and into her office. And there she saw the third man. He was dressed in a white shirt and dark slacks that looked brand-new, and his left arm was in a sling. His pale face was etched with lines of pain.

Amelia stared in shocked disbelief. Her brain wouldn't work. It had frozen at the moment she'd first met the injured man's eyes.

She felt blood drain from her face. Her dad, who'd come in right behind her, took her hand and squeezed it.

"Don't faint, daughter," he whispered. Then he stepped back outside the door and closed it, leaving her alone with Cole.

Cole. "Oh—" she mouthed.

He braced his good hand on the back of a chair. "Hi, Amelia. I'm not too steady on my feet yet," he said quietly. "You look good."

"I—I'm…" She couldn't speak. Her hands went to her mouth. Tears rolled down her cheeks. It was too much to take in.

"You were dead," she sobbed. "They covered you up. They took you away. Why didn't you tell me?"

His eyes turned dark as storm clouds. "For a while there, things didn't look too promising."

She nodded. "You lost so much blood."

"You saved my life."

A smile began to grow through her tears. "I just held on."

"Like you promised."

She touched his face. "You're really here. Really alive. Really a hero."

He caught her hand in his. "Not a hero," he said, kissing her fingers. "I'm actually nobody."

"Nobody?" Amelia didn't care what he was saying. All she wanted to do was to grab him and hold on. Nobody would ever take him away from her again. Not and live to talk about it.

"Since I was too stubborn to die, the government has put me in the witness protection program. So Cole Robinson is dead. He's gone forever." He gave her a tentative smile. "Would you consider marrying a nobody, Amelia? A nobody who's moving to Raven's Cliff to maybe work on boats?"

Amelia stepped closer to Cole and he wrapped his good arm around her. She heard a sound, like a soft laugh carried on a breeze, and the faint scent of roses wafted across her nostrils.

She put her arms around his neck and stood on tiptoe to whisper in his ear. "Just like the fortune-teller told me, *nobody* is good enough for me."

Epilogue

Camille Wells had a terrific headache. She tried to touch her temple, but her hand wouldn't move. She opened her eyes. She was in bed in a dark room, with white sheets tucked around her middle. She looked at her hand. There was an IV stuck in her wrist.

What the heck had happened to her?

Fear. Falling. Pain. The memories buffeted her confused brain.

She recalled walking along the beautiful cliff face on her father's arm. Her wedding day.

Then suddenly a gust of wind had caught her veil— and try as she might, her mind yielded up nothing else. Nothing but darkness and pain.

She must have fallen. She'd ruined the beautiful wedding her parents had been so thrilled about.

Through the sheer curtains at the window, she saw a pink glow. Sunrise. The sky was too dark for it to be sunset.

She tried to push herself up in the bed, but she couldn't. She was too weak. With a frustrated moan, she laid her head back against the pillow.

A movement in the darkest corner of the room startled her.

"Who's there?" she tried to say. Her lips moved but no sound emerged.

The shadows in the corner coalesced into a silhouette. It was a person—a man.

"Who—?" she tried again.

"Don't speak," came a hoarse whisper. "You're dreaming. Sleep. Sleep."

The room was growing brighter by the second. Camille made out a dark coat, or cloak. Before she could blink enough to clear her vision, the figure drifted toward the door and disappeared.

"Wait—" she croaked, but it was no use.

Whoever had been sitting vigil near her bedside, he was gone now. Her eyes drifted shut.

SOMETHING WAS HURTING HER EYES. Camille squinted against the bright light coming from the window. She lifted her hand—or tried to.

A snippet of memory tickled the edge of her brain. Bed. An IV. And a mysterious figure.

Her eyes flew open, and she met the startled gaze of her father.

"Dad?" Her lips moved but nothing came out.

"Camille? Oh, my little girl!" He vaulted out of the chair beside her bed and grasped her hand. "Don't try to move. Don't try to talk."

"What's going on?" Camille tried to say. She couldn't talk. She squeezed her dad's hand but he pulled it away.

"I have to get your mother—and the doctor."

"Dad, wait!" Still nothing but a barely audible croak.

The sun was high in the sky. High enough to shine directly into her eyes.

Earlier it had barely risen. Earlier? Her head hurt. What had she been dreaming? Why had she thought a dark-cloaked figure had slipped from her room as the pink glow from the window chased the shadows across the floor?

Her mother rushed into the room, followed by her father and a doctor.

"Camille, sweetheart." Her mother leaned over and planted a brief, gentle kiss on her cheek. Tears shone in her eyes.

Why was everybody acting so strange? Treating her so delicately?

"Mom?" At least this time, she'd managed an actual word. What had happened to her throat? She frowned at her mother.

"Oh, darling, don't worry about a thing. It's all right. The doctor told us everything." Her mother patted her hand. "We're just happy to have you back with us."

The doctor asked her mother and dad to leave the room for a few minutes while he examined her.

"Doctor, what—"

"Don't try to talk, Miss Wells. You've been unconscious for a long time. It's going to take a while for your voice to come back."

Unconscious?

"I've had a therapist working with your arms and legs, but as soon as you feel up to it, we need to get you up and moving about."

To her surprise, he pressed on her belly. "Now, tell me. Does that hurt? Are you sore?"

"I don't understand. What am I doing here?" Her throat hurt. It rasped, as if she hadn't used her voice in a long time. "And who was that man?"

"That man?" The doctor frowned at her. "That was your father. Young lady, do you know your name?"

"Of course I do," she whispered. "I mean, the other man—"

The door to her room opened again. It was Police Chief Swanson.

Now what?

"Doctor, I just got word that Camille was awake. I need to talk to her."

"She shouldn't be talking right now," the doctor said. "It'll probably be another day or so before she gets her voice back completely."

Chief Swanson's sharp eyes narrowed. "Well, Camille, you've got yourself into a peck of trouble now, haven't you?"

Camille stared at him.

"I told you, Chief, I don't want her talking."

"Fine. But you can hear, can't you, Camille?" The chief shooed the doctor out of the room and sat in the chair next to her hospital bed. "And you can nod, too, right?"

Camille's head was throbbing again. She squeezed her eyes shut.

"Can't you?" The chief's voice rose.

She opened her eyes and nodded gingerly.

"Good." Chief Swanson sat forward. "Why don't you tell me where your baby is?"

Baby?

Camille's left hand went to her belly and she looked

down. It felt swollen. When she realized that, she realized her breasts were tender, too. Tender and heavy.

She raised her gaze to Chief Swanson's. "I don't know what's happening," she whispered.

"Look, Camille. I know you've been unconscious, but you just had a baby, and I need to find out where it is. It's safe, isn't it? We sure don't need another death around Raven's Cliff."

"Baby? I just had a baby?" She felt tears welling in her eyes. "What do you mean? I can't have had a baby."

Something awful had happened to her. Something indescribably horrible. And she had no idea what it was.

Chief Swanson just studied her without speaking.

"Tell me what you're talking about."

"Do you know what day it is?" he asked. "What month?"

Camille rubbed her temple in confusion. "No. I mean, my wedding was in May. How long has it…how can I have had a baby?" Sobs crawled up her throat. "I want to see my mother."

"Camille, it's October. That means you were pregnant on your wedding day. Now listen to me, young lady. Whatever you remember, you'd better tell me. Because there's a tiny baby out there somewhere—all alone. *Your* baby. And you're the only person who knows where it is."

* * * * *

Don't miss the gripping conclusion of
THE CURSE OF RAVEN'S CLIFF *next month
with* Motive: Secret Baby *from Debra Webb and
Mills & Boon® Intrigue.*

Mills & Boon® Intrigue
brings you a sneak preview of …

Debra Webb's Motive: Secret Baby

*Someone has taken Camille Wells's baby. Now
it's up to sexy recluse Nicholas Sterling III to help
the woman he once loved and right his
past wrongs if he is to save the town of
Raven's Cliff from disaster…*

Don't miss this thrilling conclusion to
THE CURSE OF RAVEN'S CLIFF
*mini-series available next month from
Mills & Boon® Intrigue.*

Motive: Secret Baby

by

Debra Webb

The waves crashed ferociously against the rocky shore, sending a salty mist spraying over his bare back. The cool, damp sand beneath his arms felt familiar and comforting. But it was the woman in his arms that filled his heart and soul with longing, and at the same time with torment. Nicholas Sterling III stared into the eyes of the woman he held so tightly.

The woman with whom he had made slow, passionate love for the last time.

How could he never hold her this way again? How could he pretend what they shared meant nothing and go on with his life?

Agony squeezed his heart. Yet he must. He had an obligation. His family had arranged his marriage, his whole life. Starting tomorrow. There was no way to stop the momentum. He was to marry the chosen bride and settle into his arranged future or lose everything. His family...his inheritance. To defy his family's wishes would be to exile himself from Raven's Cliff and all that he knew.

Did he not possess the courage to start over somewhere else on his own? With nothing?

Nicholas pushed away the thought. Perhaps he was a coward. It was far too late to delve into a self-analysis. Tomorrow he would do as his family demanded.

But tonight was his. His and Camille's.

One last night to hold her. Nicholas dipped his head and tasted her sweet lips once more. Camille whimpered softly. She loved him. He knew she did.

And he loved her…desperately.

Unfortunately love was not enough.

He stilled. The bitterness of regret tainted his soul despite his determination to put all but this moment aside. The truth was, what he was doing now was unfair to Camille. Unfair to the woman he was to marry and to his family.

Those damned obligations.

This was a hell of a time for his conscience to decide it worked after all. Not once had he ever let anyone else's expectations block his path, so why tonight?

What made this night different from all the others that had come before it?

Just because in less than twenty-four hours he was scheduled to wed a woman his family had hand-picked for him…just because…

Doom crashed down around him as if lightning

had struck with unerring force. An overwhelming sense of loss pressed against his chest.

Tonight…was *the* night.

"Dear God…" He'd forgotten to go to the lighthouse.

"What's wrong?" Camille wiggled out of his arms and scooted up to a sitting position. "Nicholas?"

His gaze met hers and in a single instant he saw his true destiny reflected there. *Death.*

"I have to go." Nicholas scrambled to his feet, jerked on his jeans. "I'm sorry. I—"

"Please tell me what's wrong." Draping her abandoned dress over her bare breasts, she stared up at him, her eyes wide with worry and sadness…with her own regret. This was their last time together.

For a moment he couldn't move. He wanted so badly to take her into his arms again…to promise her whatever necessary to banish the sadness in those blue eyes.

How had he allowed his life to come to this place where nothing was as it should be?

A deafening whoosh blasted the night air, shattering the thick, tense silence. Nicholas lifted his face to the night, scanned the craggy cliff above their secluded, sandy haven.

Flames danced, illuminating the dark velvet sky.

"The lighthouse…" Apprehension tightened its noose on his neck.

He had to hurry. Before it was too late.

Nicholas ran, skirted the rocky shore his feet

knew by heart until he reached the narrow path that ascended the jagged cliff side.

His grandfather had warned him not to forget.

But Nicholas had shirked that obligation as he had most put before him.

Now he was too late.

Way too late.

The designated time had come and gone.

Dread constricted his lungs, making it difficult to breathe.

What had he done?

As he reached the summit, found his balance on the ledge that overlooked the restless ocean below, his worst fears were realized.

The lighthouse was on fire…the upper portion—the watch room where the lantern waited…*unlit*—glowed with the destructive fingers of fire.

A new kind of panic seized his heart.

"Grandfather!"

Though Nicholas had ignored his duty, his grandfather never would. Nicholas charged toward the lighthouse, flung open the door and mounted the steep, winding stairs two at a time.

"Grandfather!"

When he bounded up the final step his heart lurched. The watch room was almost completely engulfed. A kerosene can was overturned near the lantern. His grandfather lay on the floor beside it. Nicholas rushed to the motionless old man and dropped to his knees.

"Grandfather, it's okay. I'm here now." He lifted the old man into his arms.

Unseeing eyes peered up at him. Anguish tore at Nicholas's soul.

"No!" The scream echoed around him. The flames crept closer. Nicholas didn't care. His grandfather was dead and it was his fault.

"No. No. No." Desperate, Nicholas attempted CPR. "Breathe," he demanded between the puffs of air he forced into the unresponsive lungs.

Splitting glass screeched above the roar of the devouring blaze.

Nicholas glanced up at the lantern. The glass had shattered. He surveyed the wall of glass surrounding the watch room, then the floor where jagged shards had been spewed across it. The heat from the flames, he realized. The fire had swept a full circle around him.

He peered down at his grandfather. "I'm sorry," he murmured. "I'm so sorry."

Ice abruptly rushed through Nicholas's veins. His gaze was drawn back to the lantern as if a voice had whispered from it. The precious gemstones suddenly glistened, reflecting the light of the savage flames. Words gleamed across the metal of the lantern's casement—words he had never noticed before.

Fire and ice…life and death…look into your heart.

Confusion and misery made Nicholas's head spin.

He had killed his grandfather…destroyed the light-house…he was responsible…all of this was his fault.

Now is not the time to give up…there is still hope.

A force Nicholas could not name drew him to his feet…drew him to the lantern.

I pray the hollows my soul to keep.

Nicholas could almost hear his grandfather's voice reciting the silly childhood prayer….

His grandfather lay still, unmoving on the floor.

This didn't make sense. Nicholas was delusional. Did one lose his mind in those final moments before death claimed him?

Now I lay me down to sleep.

"Stop!" Nicholas put his hands over his ears. This couldn't be real.

I pray the hollows my soul to keep.

A frantic cry from far below snapped Nicholas from the baffling trance he'd slipped into. He coughed. Smoke had invaded deep into his lungs.

Another desperate cry.

Camille.

She shouted his name from the ground below.

If she tried to come up the stairs after him…too dangerous.

He would not be responsible for her death as well.

Summoning the courage that had deserted him in his misery, he shouted, "Get help!" Nicholas rushed back to where his grandfather lay and hefted him into his arms. He tried to dart through the flames to reach the stairs, but it was impossible. The entire upper portion of the staircase was swallowed up by the devouring blaze.

Defeat sucked at Nicholas's trembling limbs. There was no escape.

He was going to die.

Nicholas peered down at his beloved grandfather.

This was Nicholas's fault. He deserved to die.

And Raven's Cliff will die with you.

He jerked with a start at the words.

Where had that voice come from?

He turned all the way around. The fire had trapped him. Yet, there was no one else, except his grandfather, who could have spoken to him.

Nicholas shook his head. He was hearing things again. His jaw hardened as sweat ran down his bare skin. *You deserve to die,* he reminded himself and the voice.

Yes, he deserved no better than this.

Cradling his grandfather, Nicholas dropped to his knees to await his fate.

He heard the voice again. *The riddle is the key to salvation...to reversing the curse.*

Nicholas closed his eyes and shook his head. The heat...had to be the heat. He was going to die. He was imagining the voice. He didn't believe in the curse. He didn't believe in anything.

If you die...Raven's Cliff will die, too.

In the Sheikh's power

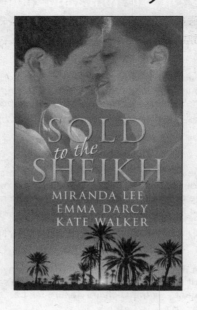

Be tempted by three seductive Sheikhs in:

Love-Slave to the Sheikh by Miranda Lee
Traded to the Sheikh by Emma Darcy
At the Sheikh's Command by Kate Walker

Available 5th June 2009

FREE!

2 Books
and a surprise gift!

We would like to take this opportunity to thank you for reading this Mills & Boon® book by offering you the chance to take TWO more specially selected titles from the Intrigue series absolutely FREE! We're also making this offer to introduce you to the benefits of the Mills & Boon® Book Club™—

- ★ **FREE home delivery**
- ★ **FREE gifts and competitions**
- ★ **FREE monthly Newsletter**
- ★ **Exclusive Mills & Boon Book Club offers**
- ★ **Books available before they're in the shops**

Accepting these FREE books and gift places you under no obligation to buy, you may cancel at any time, even after receiving your free shipment. Simply complete your details below and return the entire page to the address below. You don't even need a stamp!

YES! Please send me 2 free Intrigue books and a surprise gift. I understand that unless you hear from me, I will receive 4 superb new titles every month for just £3.19 each, postage and packing free. I am under no obligation to purchase any books and may cancel my subscription at any time. The free books and gift will be mine to keep in any case.

19ZEF

Ms/Mrs/Miss/Mr ....Initials ....

Surname .... **BLOCK CAPITALS PLEASE**

Address...

....

....Postcode ....

Send this whole page to:
UK: FREEPOST CN81, Croydon, CR9 3WZ